Highland Daydreams

The MacKinnon Clan Series
Book Three

April Holthaus

Edited by: One More Time Editing LLC
Cover Design by: Leanne Edwards
Printed in the United States
First Printing: September 2014
ISBN-10: 1500179124
ISBN-13: 978-1500179120
All rights reserved.

Dedication

This book is dedicated to the Sandberg Family of Minneapolis, Minnesota (descendants of Carl and Helen). I would not be the person I am today if it were not for my family.

To my husband and son, your love and support encourage me to reach for my dreams!

Acknowledgement

I would like to give a special thanks to all of my readers and Facebook friends. Your support and encouragement have been greatly appreciated. Thank you for taking a chance on me!

I would also like to send out a special thank you to my beta readers who have helped make this book be the best it can be! Thank you, Nicole Laverdure, Jennifer Green, Kimberly Court, Barbara Cooch, Rhonda Kirby, Maria McIntyre, and Stephanie Kennedy! And of course, Thanks to Helen, my editor for all of the last minute details and changes!

Content

Prologue

July 22, 1298
Falkirk, Scotland

The sky darkened. Rain had fallen for more than an hour causing the ground to become slippery and muddy beneath Bram's feet. Holding his sword high, he waited for Wallace's battle cry. His breaths became labored and each exhale more intense. The noises around him were muffled over the sound of his heart beating loudly in his ears. Squeezing his grip tighter to steady the hilt of his broadsword, he waited. Clutching the strap of his shield, he pulled it firmly against his chest. Over the assembly of men and commotion, a call echoed.

A sea of men on each side of him barreled down the hill toward their enemy. Bram had no time to think and he acted on instinct alone. Thrashing his sword, he cut down the first few men charging towards him from the left and then the right. He raised his shield when the whistling sound of falling arrows came closer and louder but he did not slow his pace. He used his shield to push past a group of warriors to advance further towards his enemy.

For a brief moment, Bram stood in the middle of a clearing. Men had fought and fallen around him; both comrade and enemy. With eyes looking wildly about at the scene before him, he searched for his next victim. To his right, a soldier dressed in chainmail ran towards him. Sword drawn, he yelled out all sorts of blasphemies. Lowering his weapon with the blade directed towards Bram, the soldier readied himself to slice Bram through.

Bram turned to fight off another opponent, who violently swung his sword harder and harder, forcing Bram to take short steps backwards. Bram leapt to the side, able to dodge the first blow, but met the second with the pure force of his blade. A forceful shot to Bram's ribs sent ripples of pain throughout his body. He cried out in agony. Dropping to his knees, Bram wrapped one of his arms tightly around his chest and attempted to rise. But just as he was about to stand, the man took a sharp dirk out of his boot and slashed it across Bram's abdomen.

Bram could feel the heat of the blade as it sliced through his skin down to the muscle. Blood spilled down the front of him. Unexpectedly, a sudden dizzy spell overcame him. Bram doubled over and fell into a small puddle. Lying on the ground, he waited for death to take him. His eyes closed, the blackness came, and then there was nothing but silence.

Chapter 1

August, 1298
Cumberland, England

Dragging the heavy weight of the iron chain secured to her ankle, Lara scurried across the floor of her cell. She tucked her knees under her chin, and wrapped her arms securely around her legs, sitting quiet and still. As her stomach growled once more, Lara pressed her hands firmly against her stomach, wishing away her hunger. The boniness of her ribs beneath her hands told her that if she did not die of illness, she would certainly die of starvation.

Lara was uncertain if it had been weeks or months she had spent within the bowels of the dungeon, for time did not exist within the darkness. She could no longer hear the desperate cries of her fellow cell mates, nor could she feel her own wounds or pains.

Lara hid her face within the folds of what was left of her dress when she heard the guards making their way down the stone stairwell. As they entered this room in the dungeon, they yelled profanities at a prisoner they dragged with them.

They threatened that if he didn't walk faster they would pitch him down the stairs.

She felt her body quiver with fear when she spied Roland, the heavier of the two guards. Roland had once visited Lara in her cell trying to satisfy his needs before he was reprimanded by another guard and forced back out of her cell. Angered by Roland's attempted rape, the Earl of Cumberland had struck him so hard it created a grotesque scar across his face that left him almost unrecognizable.

Since that wretched day, Roland accused Lara for what had happened, swearing that he would take his revenge out on her. He often tried to put the fear of God in her with his abhorrent threats. At times, Lara wished he would just get it over with so he would leave her alone.

As he entered, Roland peeked around the bars and gave her a half smile. Lara looked away and clasped onto the hem of her skirt a little tighter. Roland turned and instructed the other guard to string up their prisoner by his wrists. The man stumbled forward as the guards dragged him to a wooden pole where a thick rope dangled from a beam on the ceiling. Wrapping the rope around his wrists, the guard tied the knot tightly. The prisoner was hoisted up and stretched from limb to limb.

11

When they turned him to expose his bare back, the side of his face became visible in the soft light of the torch on the wall. It was *him*. He was the only one who never fought back or struggled when the guards came for him. Lara was unsure where his unbreakable strength came from, but knew that only a warrior could be so brave. The only spark of life Lara had left within her was the empathy she felt for this warrior who shared the cell next to hers. Lara shuddered as the crack of the whip bit into the man's flesh. The prisoners around her yelled in the man's defense, but no sound came from the captive himself. He just clenched his teeth and endured the pain. Lara could not tell how many times they struck him for she tried to block it out.

In a chilling and raspy voice Roland demanded that he be cut down. Lifting her head up, Lara watched as the warrior hung from the rafter, limp, his head hanging to one side. Sweat and blood glistened off his body. The guard took his blade out of its sheath and sliced the rope in two. In that instant, the warrior plummeted to the ground. The portly guard picked him up by his arms and began to drag him back into his cell.

"Get in there!" the guard roared as he shoved him inside the small space.

Roland held him down as the warrior was once again chained to the wall in iron shackles.

Still curled up in the corner, Lara looked at him through the bars, tears streaming down her face. He looked broken, not only physically, but in spirit as well. She carefully watched the guards as they returned to their posts. She knew that one of them would head back up the stairs with the others while her tormentor would sit down on his chair outside her cell, tilt it back against the bars and slam back a tankard or two of whiskey. Their routine had become predictable the last several nights, and Lara had taken notice.

"Hello, my beauty," Roland whispered to her through the cell bars, so low that no one else could hear him.

His breath smelled like rotten food and stale ale.

"My body is aching for the sweetness between your thighs and I promise that you will enjoy it," he threatened.

"Perhaps ye would like a matching scar across the other side of yer face," she threatened.

Roland chuckled.

"Oh how I love a woman with some fight in her."

Lara looked away from him and hugged her knees tighter into her chest. She prayed God would take her from this place. She would rather die than stay here another night. Resting her head upon her knees, she chewed her bottom lip, in an effort to keep herself from falling asleep. If she were to drift off, she would be left vulnerable, and Roland would surely have his way with her. It would be no different than what had been done to her by that despicable man Dermot, her *husband*.

Married for no more than a sennight, Lara was still angry with herself for believing his sweet and flowery words. She had become so easily blinded by hope that she missed the obvious signs of treachery. She, like her father, had believed that the marriage of Lara and Dermot would end years of feuds between their clans. By uniting them there should have been peace. That is what Errol, Laird of Clan Moray swore his life upon with his very last breath; but no, in truth, his son Dermot proved to be a most vicious and vile man. He had chosen not to keep his father's promise. But still, she never could have imagined that *this* would have happened.

As if it were yesterday, she recalled the morning she pleaded with her father to void the contract and marry her off to another; any other.

14

She had only met Dermot once, many years ago, but his rude and selfish behavior left a bitter taste in her mouth. Having to marry him made Lara's stomach twist and churn.

"Lara, ye are meddling in things in which ye should nay be meddling. Ye are ten and seven years old. 'Tis time ye were married," her father croaked.

"Meddling? Is my life no' my business? I will do my duty and marry the swine. But ye are sacrificing me to the wolves. How do ye ken ye can trust 'em? Even their own priest had been condemned for treason. The Morays' have ne'er kept their word or their promises. Surely ye can find me a better suitor and our clan a better ally."

Her father's eyes darkened like the night sky and his brows furrowed. In a deep and lowered tone he replied, "We need this alliance, Lara. We have far too many enemies. Ye will do the Laird's bidding if he so wishes it. Ye will marry the son of Laird Moray and that is the end of it. Ye will no' defy me again. I have found ye a suitor who has the means to care fer ye. God only hope he can handle ye. I will no' hear another word."

Lara's thoughts were interrupted by a loud snore coming from outside her cell. With the

15

guard asleep, Lara was sure that this time she would be able to slip her thin, bony wrists out of the shackles without notice. Lara reached out and wet her wrists from a small puddle of muddy water that had been leaking from the ceiling onto the ground. She began to vigorously twist her right hand back and forth successfully popping it out of its binding. Repeating the same thing with the other hand, she was able to free herself from the irons. Now she only needed the key to unlock the one around her ankle.

Glancing around the room, she saw no one had noticed her actions, except for the nameless warrior whose heavy gaze sent chills down Lara's spine. He watched her like a hawk watching his prey, but remained silent. On her hands and knees, Lara silently crawled towards Roland. Sliding her small hands through the bars, she slipped Roland's dagger from his belt. With one forceful thrust, she stabbed the man in the back.

Roland howled in agony. Lara twisted the blade and pulled it back out as blood gushed from his wound. It took only moments before his body became motionless and fell from his chair onto the ground. Lara promised herself that she would not mourn this loss of life though she would be dutiful and ask God for forgiveness.

Lara's arm ached as she stretched it as far as she could through the bars for the key ring latched to his belt. Once she retrieved it, she removed her ankle chain, staggered to the door of her cell, and swung the door open. The loud creak of steel echoed throughout the chamber. The prisoners around her had remained silent until now. Whispering in low voices they begged for her to help release them, but her time was precious and she knew that she could not save them all.

With little time to escape, Lara crept towards the stairs. Putting one foot on the first step, she felt an unnerving tightness in her chest. She looked back over her shoulder to the injured warrior. His body was slumped to one side and his worn out arms hung lifeless from the chains. Seeing his helplessness, she knew she had to save him. She could not let a man as brave as he, die in here. Inspired by his valor and strength, Lara took courage. If it were not for him, she may never have had the bravery to take a man's life to save her own.

Quickly, but as quiet as a field mouse, she ran to his cell, turned the key in the lock, and unlatched the door. The warrior raised his head to her but said nothing. For a fleeting moment, Lara wondered if perhaps the warrior was a mute. For the past two weeks, he had not said one word. From above the staircase, Lara heard a noise from the guards. Worried that her escape would fail, she tossed the key ring at his side and prayed her small token of freedom would help him escape as well. Lara took off running up the long staircase.

Once she reached the top step, Lara looked around and saw two guards sitting at a small round table in heavy debate. Their distraction and conversation made it easy for Lara to take the opportunity to examine the large open room. On each side of the room were two wooden support beams that held up the ceiling; just wide enough for Lara to hide behind, unnoticed, if she could get to them. When the guards weren't looking, she held her breath and quickly advanced forward to the first beam.

Pressing her back up against the first beam, she waited to see if the guards had noticed her presence. She could feel her chest rise and fall with each unsteady breath. Lara felt her knees start to buckle and she could not stop her hands from shaking. After a few minutes, she peeked around the wooden beam to see if all was clear. The guards continued to be distracted. Taking in another deep breath, she ran as quietly and swiftly as she could to the next one, stepping as light as a feather.

Lara could feel the hairs on her arms rise and her heartbeat quicken. She had made it this far and now freedom was only a few more feet away. She prayed her attempt would be successful and not in vain. It had been a long while since she breathed in the crisp, fresh air and felt the earth beneath her feet. She was determined to do so again even if she had to kill every guard that stood in her way.

As soon as she was able to look back at the guards, Lara heard the jingling sound of a chain coming from the stairs that led to the dungeon. The guards jumped from their chairs and ran over to the staircase to inspect the noise. Lara used the distraction to run to the alcove which framed the door.

Carefully, she began to turn the handle.

"What do you think you are doing?" one of the guards yelled from across the room.

Lara panicked; so frightened her body went stiff. Unexpectedly, she heard a loud painful moan followed by several grunts and heavy breathing from behind her. Looking over her shoulder, she saw the two guards engaged in a brawl with the nameless warrior who had managed to escape his cell as well. A crack to the jaw, a jab to the stomach, the warrior fell to his knees. His two attackers circled around and mocked him for his failed attempt to escape.

Lara's heart ached for him. He was in no condition to fight. But just as she thought his luck had run out, the warrior grabbed onto the back of one of the guard's knees and pummeled him to the ground. Bringing his fist up high into the air, he swung down making contact with the guard's nose knocking him out cold. Blood trickled down the guard's face and spilled onto the floor.

The other guard grabbed onto the warrior's arms, but the warrior twisted his upper body, tossing the man over his shoulder and slamming him onto the ground. After a few more swings and punches, the warrior was able to render the second guard unconscious as well.

Lara could feel goose bumps creep along her arms as the warrior limped toward her. He was taller than she had expected. From the dim light, all she could tell was that he had long hair with a matching beard, broad shoulders and a thin waistline. Still unable to make out his features, she watched as he looked past her out the door.

"Run towards the trees, and follow me close. I dinna want to lose ye," he whispered, as he pushed her through the door and started running towards the dense forest.

Chapter 2

The blackness of night blinded Lara from seeing the low branches as she ran past them. Small twigs slashed across her face, stinging her cheeks. Too dark to see even a few feet ahead of her, Lara was uncertain where they were heading. Deep inside, she wanted to trust him, but still had reservations. Even though they had shared more than a week together in the same hellish pit, she knew nothing of him. And she had no cause or reason to trust him.

Even with the warrior's obvious injuries, Lara had a hard time keeping up with him. He was fast and physically in better shape than she was. The muscles in her legs started to burn. She knew not how she could keep going. Let the English come, she thought. Tripping over small tree roots on the forest floor, Lara tumbled forward, collapsing to her knees. The warrior ran back to her.

"Are ye hurt?" he asked.

Lara shook her head.

"Nay. Go. Just leave me, please," she begged as tears flowed freely down her cheeks.

"Nay. Now get up," he said as he grabbed under her arms, helping her to her feet. "Ye canna stop. Ye must keep going."

Lara took a deep breath and nodded her head.

Silently, they trotted through the forest for miles within the dark until they came across a campfire where three men were sleeping. The campfire burned low and the men snored loudly, covering the sound of leaves crunching under Lara's feet. The warrior put his finger to his lips indicating for Lara to keep quiet as he crept further towards them. He stopped and waited for several long moments. Holding his hand up for Lara to stay where she was, he walked to the other side of their camp where three horses were tied to a tree.

Without a word, he gave Lara a wave of his hand for her to walk towards him. Lara's heart raced. She had to put her hand over her mouth to quiet her breathing. Her legs felt like dough and shook almost uncontrollably at the knees. She stepped lightly, praying to God that she could make it across the campsite without waking the men. As she walked towards her companion, her eyes did not stray from the sleeping men. That was her first mistake. Stepping on a twig, she gasped and felt her heart drop in her chest. Lara froze in place. She was no longer able to quiet her breathing as she imagined all sort of terrible things the men would do to them once they discovered their presence. She couldn't move, she couldn't think; her head began to spin. The warrior calmly walked back towards Lara and took her by the hand. Together they walked to the other side of the camp. Lara took a sigh of relief when they safely made it across. Grabbing onto her waist, he carefully lifted Lara on top of one of the horses. The horse grunted loudly.

"What is that?" a man grumbled as he looked in Lara's and the warrior's direction. "Wake up ye eejits, they are stealing our horses!" he hollered.

With lightning speed, the warrior untied the ropes, freeing the other two horses. Swinging up behind her and wrapping one arm around her waist, he grabbed onto the reigns. After a loud slap to the horse's rump, the horse bolted into a fast sprint. The men's voices from behind them began to fade as the distance between them and the camp increased.

After riding several hours, Lara could smell the distinct aroma of food being carried on the wind. The delectable smell made her stomach growl and mouth water. The warrior slowed the horse and stilled its movement as they came upon a small dwelling.

The croft was made of stone and looked as if it had been abandoned. Several stones had crumbled showing signs of erosion and the ill-thatched roof was in desperate need of repair. Along the back side of the croft was a small barn that housed two horses and throughout the yard a dozen chickens pecked the ground.

At first, her instinct was to tell him to keep going for she did not know if they were on English soil or Scotland's. However, the smell of the food and the idea of a warm pallet were far too tempting. As they drew closer towards the barn, the chickens became startled by the horse and began to cluck loudly.

"Who goes there?" a woman croaked.

"I apologize, my lady, I dinna mean to disturb ye," the warrior replied.

Once the woman came into view, the warrior dismounted and walked closer to her but remained in the shadows. The woman was old with a round mid-section and stood half as tall as him. Her clothes were tattered and worn and her silvery hair was partially covered by a white linen head-rail.

"Are ye the mon, McGregor sent lookin' fer work? I was told that ye would no' be here fer a few days."

"Nay, my lady. I am no' McGregor. We are passing through and happened to come across yer lands. We are seeking food and shelter."

Lara watched as the old woman looked the warrior up and down. Tilting her head to the side, she looked behind him to Lara who was still perched on top of the horse. Pursing her lips, the woman looked at the two of them very carefully.

"Have ye any coin?" she rudely asked.

"Nay, my lady," the warrior replied.

"Well, if ye cannae pay me then ye will work fer yer meal."

"Of course, my lady," the warrior said, and slightly bowed his head to her.

"And who is that there wit ye?" she asked.

"Only an acquaintance, my lady."

"Well, come here so I can have a look at ye," she insisted.

Lara slid down the side of the horse and slowly came out of the shadow and stood within the light of the moon. With her hands balled tightly against her sides, she readied herself to run if instinct told her to. Her stomach clenched when the old woman gazed down at her with beady eyes. The woman expressed a look of astonishment as if she was utterly appalled by Lara's appearance.

Keeping her arms close to her sides, Lara kept her head lowered. Ashamed of her ragged dress and nappy hair, Lara bit her bottom lip hoping not to be ridiculed by the woman.

"Good God lass, what happened to ye?

Lara did not know how to respond. She knew nothing of this woman nor whether she could be trusted. She certainly could not tell the woman who she was and from where she had just escaped. Lara remained silent. Glancing over to the warrior, she looked for some indication as to what to do or say to the old hag but he stood quiet, staring at her blankly. In the dim light of dusk, she could only feel his stare.

"What is yer name?" she asked rather impatiently. "Well now, dinna be shy. Speak up lass."

"Lara," she quietly responded, giving the woman nothing more than her first name.

"It's good to meet ye, Lara. My name is Rowena," she said, then turned her attention back to the warrior. "The lass can sleep inside. As fer ye, there should be plenty of hay fer ye in the barn. Tomorrow mornin' I expect ye to have the horses brushed down and the chickens fed. When my husband, Innes, returns in the mornin' he can tell ye what else needs to be done. He works as a blacksmith in the village so he is away often. We lost our last farmhand, so much is needed to be done. If ye prove to be well worth the hire, I shall e'en pay ye," the woman offered to the warrior.

"Thank ye, my lady," he said in a more grateful tone.

Lara followed Rowena towards the front of the house. Before turning the corner, the woman turned back and asked, "Laddie, what do I call ye?"

The warrior cleared his throat before speaking.

"Bram, my lady. My name is Bram MacKinnon."

Grateful for the woman's hospitality, Bram eagerly walked towardss the barn. He welcomed the fresh air and a dry pallet. The past two weeks had been hell on both his body and his mind. As he entered the barn, he noted a stack of hay in one of the abandoned stalls. Grabbing a large heap of it, he arranged the hay into flat layers on the ground. Bram laid his weary body down upon a wool sack he had found and placed on top of the hay. He swore to the heavens that he would forever lie in that spot and not move another muscle.

Rolling to his side and placing his arm underneath his head, his muscles twitched as pain shot down his right arm and lower back. He yearned for a tankard of whiskey to drink away his pain or knock him out completely. His body felt as if he had been tied up and dragged by a horse running at full speed.

Stretching his arms wide, he rubbed his shoulders to loosen his tense muscles. Carefully, he lifted the blood-stained tunic over his head and tossed it onto the ground; his back still sore from the lashings. Lying back, he tried to close his eyes for just a bit but his effort failed miserably.

Overly exhausted, Bram knew he needed to rest, but sleep eluded him. It was the silence that plotted against him, denying him the rest he so desperately needed. For every time he closed his eyes; he was back on the battlefield. The flashbacks were vivid; waking nightmares. The sound of metal clashing, the buzzing of arrows whizzing through the air and the smell of death all around him. But it wasn't actually the battle that haunted him. In all of his twenty three years, he had been in battle many times and not once had it changed him. But a pair of dark blue eyes belonging to an English soldier haunted his dreams. Those eyes belonged to the man who had pierced his sword into Bram's abdomen causing him to lose so much blood it rendered him unconscious.

Bram hoped fate would allow him to face that man again someday. Looking down at his stomach, he saw the ghastly scar that was still continuing to heal. He could still feel the heat of the Englishman's blade every time he looked at it; a memory not so easily forgotten.

The imprisonment he endured was nothing compared to witnessing his Scottish brethren slaughtered that rainy day. Bram felt he should have been among them. He recalled the heavy rainfall washing the blood and mud away from his face. He was shaken awake and carried off in a wagon pulled by two black horses draped in the English royal colors until he awoke in the dungeons at Cumberland.

Bram had expected his execution to come quick, but the Earl of Cumberland had delayed the trials while he was attending the marriage of his cousin, the Duke of York, to Lady Rosalind of

Northumberland. Bram learned many valuable things while listening to the guards talk amongst each other; things he was most anxious to rely back to William Wallace and Robert the Bruce. But most importantly, to his own brother, Rory, Laird of Clan MacKinnon.

Over and over, Bram struggled with why his cousin Ewan, who had fought aside him, had left him on the battlefield to die. When Bram had regained the strength to lift his head out of the muck, he had seen a group of his fellow Scotsmen retreat towards the woods along with Ewan. Ewan was more of a brother to him than his own brother Rory. His brother felt that Bram's adventurous temperament was more a burden than a blessing. Ewan, however, was different. He still knew how to enjoy adventure, unlike Rory. Bram knew that he could not fault Ewan for leaving him behind. He would only have left if he thought Bram was dead.

His thoughts turned to home. He missed the sights, the smells, even his overbearing brother. It had not been the first time he had been away from Dunakin Castle. In fact, he had left for weeks at a time on several occasions, gallivanting across the Highlands, meeting with the neighboring clans as well as visiting his favorite French whore, Genevieve.

How he wished to be with her now, to feel the soft touch of her bosom. To Bram, women were made for bedding and breeding. His brother Rory blamed his arrogance about women on Elspeth, a young, dark-haired maiden, he'd once loved who had turned her attentions to Rory. Bram had thought to marry the lass, but she had broken his heart. After her untimely death he viewed marriage as a fool's game, and there were far too many women who willingly offered to lie on their backs for him without it.

Bram had never missed an opportunity to lift a lass' skirt. Even though he would leave them without words of commitment, he always accepted the consequences thereafter. He had two sons already. Colin, his oldest at seven summers, born to Marietta, and Connor, a wee laddie of four summers, to Fiona.

Never committing to either lass, Bram gratefully welcomed the bairns into his life. Thinking about his two young lads now weighed heavy on his heart. He felt full of guilt for leaving them. But he knew they were brave lads, and they would believe that their father had died heroically in battle. Still, the emptiness in his chest had him longing for home.

Chapter 3

Bram's head perked up when he heard the sound of a stick breaking under one's foot. With pure instinct, he rose, ready to defend himself. As he stood with fists tightened, Lara entered the barn holding onto a trencher of food and drink. The tray was full of dried venison, bread, and a small-sized mug of whiskey. Bram silently thanked the heavens for the whiskey.

"I thought ye might be hungry," she whispered keeping her head low as if she were a servant offering up a meal to a king.

"Aye, I am," he answered.

As he reached out for the tray, her hands began to tremble.

"I'll no' hurt ye lass," he whispered, hoping to ease her mind. Noticing that she continued to keep her head down, Bram wondered if she was afraid of him. She was not like the women that usually caught Bram's eye. This lass was scrawny, small chested, and her skin was as pale as sheep's wool. Her long black hair was a dull tangled mess.

Thinking back over the past two weeks, Bram had to admit that he had not paid much attention to her. The lass often hid in the dark corner of her cell and kept to herself. Bram knew that whatever her reason for imprisonment, it was none of his business. Only now did he begin to feel guilt and shame for not intervening on her behalf. After all, the lass had saved his life, and no woman he had ever known had shown such bravery as this daring lass had. But he accepted that he could not have saved her any more than he could have saved himself. Whatever the reason, she seemed more resilient and resourceful then he had given her credit for. And now with her cowering before him, he wondered if it was his appearance that frightened her so. Bram promised himself that before returning to his own homestead, he would safely see her home and back into the arms of her family.

Bram gently took the tray from her and set it near his pallet on the floor. He sat back down and ate every small morsel on the tray while Lara quietly stood motionless. It had been what seemed like forever since he'd had a real meal. His last food had been meat from a dead mouse the guards had given him, but it only resulted in the mouse coming back up along with the other contents of his stomach. With his belly full, and the slight relief he got from the whiskey, he looked back at Lara who was now looking at him wide-eyed as if she were witnessing a wild animal devouring its meal.

With her mouth agape, Lara stared at Bram. The moonlight shined through the barn door allowing her a better view. Hunched over on the ground, he ate as wildly as a starved animal. His eyes looked fierce yet his face displayed a look of pity. His cheeks and chin were covered by a thick tawny beard making it hard for Lara to see what he truly looked like under the mass of hair. He was bare chested wearing nothing but his kilt.

Lara did not recognize his clan because the colors were faded and worn. His bulky arms showed off his sculpted muscles and his chest had a small patch of hair that curled around over his sternum. Lara's eyes trailed lower to his stomach. At the sight of it, Lara bit her bottom lip when she saw a scar across the side of his gut that looked as if it should have taken the life from him. It was deep, still showing some areas that hadn't yet scabbed over, and would create a permanent scar. Across his shoulders were streaks of dried blood and specs of dirt and sand. She watched as he struggled to move freely.

"Ye are injured," she said as she stepped closer to him, wanting to examine his wounds.

"I am fine," he replied.

"Nay, ye are covered in blood and I am sure that yer wounds will become infected if they are not mended and washed properly," Lara insisted.

Before he could protest, Lara grabbed a rag that hung on a rusty nail and dipped it inside a bucket containing rain water. Wringing it out, she walked back to Bram and cautiously sat down next to him. Sitting so close, she could feel the heat radiate off his skin. It caused her to worry that he may already have succumbed to fever.

It was only due to her concern for him that she made the bold move. She did not know what came over her or where she gained the courage to be so presumptuous. But she had seen a great deal of battle wounds before and what happened to them when not mended properly.

"Lie down on yer stomach," she instructed.

Bram looked at her awkwardly, wondering where the quiet and shy lass had gone.

"Go on now," she ordered.

Not wanting to argue, Bram rolled over and laid flat, resting his head on his arms. Without touching him, Lara examined his wounds. She was thankful that the welts and gashes were not as bad as she had imagined, for she had no salve to put on

37

them. She lifted the cloth in her hand and gently dabbed it on his wounds. Bram winced.

"Does it hurt? I am sorry. I am trying to be as gentle as I can," Lara said, worried that the pressure she applied was too much for him to bear. She tried to press softly but perhaps he was in more pain than he would admit.

"Nay, lass. 'Tis only cold."

Lara let out a sigh of relief and continued to minister to his wounds while her other hand rested firmly on his shoulder.

"May I ask...why were ye imprisoned?" Lara whispered quietly.

She prayed it wasn't because of some evil deed such as rape or murder. She waited several moments for him to answer.

"A month or so ago, I was in Falkirk battling the English alongside William Wallace when I was injured. I was knocked unconscious and unable to defend myself. When I woke, I was bound in irons. After a week they moved me to Cumberland where ye were."

"William Wallace! Are ye a Highlander then?" she asked, though there was no doubt in her mind that he was. His muscular size, long hair, and plaid told her all she needed to know.

Her father had told her grand stories when she was young about the Highlanders; how they treated their women and favored their drinks. He said that Highlanders were selfish beasts and cared for their women like Englishmen would care for their cattle. Lara wondered if Bram would have treated her differently had she not saved him. She also wondered had she known he was a Highlander from the start whether she, too, would have made a different choice. Either way, for now all they had were each other.

"Aye, lass. I be a Highlander."

Bram kept his eyes closed tight. It was not the pain or the coolness of the water that bothered him. It was Lara's hand that had troubled him so. It was soothing and made his blood run hotter. With his head to the side he stared at her exposed legs, then to her waist, but dared not to look any higher. Bram sat up and took the cloth out of Lara's hand.

"I havnae had a chance to thank ye, but I must ask, why did ye do it? Ye risked yer life, saving mine. Ye also took a man's life, which couldnae have been easy on ye. If ye'd waited another moment or two, ye would have been caught."

"I have prayed and repented to God many times for taking that guard's life, but it was either his or mine. I saved ye because," her voice trailed off as if she was uncertain herself why she had saved him.

"Aye?" he said encouraging her to finish.

"Because of yer fearlessness. Ye withstood every lashing and still stood proud. It was yer honor and strength that I admired and I couldnae let ye die there. It was worth the risk," she replied hoping she did not sound too naïve.

"Then I owe ye my life, my lady," he vowed.

Taking her hand in his, he lifted her hand to his lips, and placed a soft kiss on the back of it. Lara quivered at his touch and quickly snatched her hand back. She was shocked that he dared to touch her so intimately.

"I make a promise to ye lass. I will do all I can to see ye safely home."

Lara smiled in return for his generous offer.

"Yer wounds are healing nicely and dinna show any sign of infection," she informed him.

"Thank ye. Ye must have much experience to ken such things. Are ye the healer in yer clan?" he asked, hoping to learn more about her.

Lara softly giggled. "Nay, I am no' a healer. My father would no' allow it but I used to watch my mother tend my father's battle wounds so I have seen much in the art of healing."

"Used to?" he asked. "Does yer mother nay longer tend to him?"

Lara's face went flat. The memory of her mother caused Lara to feel sad as if Mam had just died all over again.

"Me mother died when I was ten and two," she explained.

Bram felt guilty for asking the question. He did not mean to bring up such bad memories. Her saddened expression pulled on his heartstrings. He wanted to comfort her but knew not how to proceed. He had no experience with comforting women in loss or matters of the heart. He wondered what else the poor lass had endured. Bram turned his head and looked at her for a moment.

Wanting to change the subject and the unpleasant atmosphere his question had caused, he asked, "And what crime did ye commit against the English?"

Lara's throat constricted, causing her to swallow hard. She had hoped to avoid the question as it was too unbearable to talk about. Her lungs tightened as if the air had thinned.

In a stern voice, she replied, "I did nay such thing. My only crime was that I was powerless to stop it."

Noticing the sorrow in her voice, he apologized.

"I did no' mean to cause ye distress, my lady."

Wiping a tear away, she stood and brushed the dirt from her skirt, distracting her mind from the haunting images that crept within.

"Can I ask, why dinna yer clan or father no' come fer ye?"

"I dinna think my father kens. I nay longer live wit me father," she explained.

"Where is yer family?"

"My clan lives at Stearns Castle. My father is Laird of our clan."

"And what clan be that?"

"Clan Fergusson."

Bram began to feel uneasiness in his stomach by her revelation. The MacKinnons were not allies with the Fergusson clan nor were they allied with many of the Lowland clans. The Lowlanders had given their allegiance to the English King, Edward, Bram's people's greatest enemy.

"Who take cares of ye lass, if no' yer father?"

Bram could see hurt in her eyes from whatever image his words brought to mind. And whatever it was, it frightened her. With his thumb, he wiped away a tear that had slowly crept down her cheek. Her skin was soft under his rough, calloused hands.

"What's the matter, lass? What happened to ye?" he asked, but she gave him no reply.

Mayhap she was afraid to speak the truth. Or perhaps whoever her caregiver was, they were the one responsible for giving her over to the English. Bram silently cursed the person who had done any wrong by her.

With dread, he asked again, "Were they the ones who gave ye over to the English?"

"Aye. But I wish to no' talk about it," she said in a faint whisper.

Bram's eyebrows furrowed and a deep scowl replaced the smile on his face. How could someone do that to such a sweet, young, and innocent lass? Surely they must have known what the English would have done to her. Had he known who the person was, he would make certain that they suffered the same fate tenfold.

"I promise ye lass that ye are safe wit me. No harm will come to ye while ye are under my protection. I will make sure ye make it safely home to yer clan."

"And what of ye? Will ye return to yer family as well?"

"Aye."

"Do ye live in the far north of the Highlands?"

"Aye. Dunakin Castle is along Loch Alsh just south of the Isle of Skye. My clan settled there more than a century ago."

"And what of yer family? Yer father, yer mother?" Lara asked, curious to understand more about her docile warrior.

"My father is dead and my mother is still verra much alive. And my brother, Rory, is Laird of our clan."

"Brother? Ye are the laird's brother?" Lara asked thinking all this time that he walked the earth like a nomad, a warrior who fought for the freedom of others, never imagining that he had a family.

"Aye."

Hesitantly, she bit her lip and asked, "And yer wife?"

Bram laughed at her question.

"I be no' married lass and nay lass would want to marry me. But, I do have me two young lads, Connor and Colin."

"I apologize, I assumed."

"Tis alright."

For some reason the thought of him not being married made Lara inwardly smile.

"Ye must miss them terribly."

"Aye, I do."

Looking out the doorway, Lara thought to return inside before their hostess thought they had run off.

"I think I should return to the croft... I trust ye can finish the rest?" she said, looking at the dried blood still staining his shoulders and chest.

"Aye. Thank ye" he replied.

"Yer welcome."

Chapter 4

Hours passed. Bram lay upon his pallet trying to piece together Lara's story about how she came to be in the hands of the English. It was not very often that the English would imprison a woman in the dungeons along with the men. Imprison them, yes, but they were usually held in private rooms or in cages to be put on public display. Bram thought that she must have committed some extraordinary crime that she was unwilling to admit to be treated as such. Perhaps she'd committed treason against the king or killed an Earl. She had taken one man's life with no regard, was it conceivable that she had taken another?

It seemed impossible that she could have killed any man for that matter. If Bram had not witnessed it for himself he would never have believed it. She was a vexing and tricky wench, he thought, admiring her audacity.

With his mind racing, Bram tried to settle his thoughts. Looking around the small barn, the room was filled with hay, feed for the chickens, and four stalls; two of them had a horse in each quietly grazing on a pile of hay. He also noticed a long work table with a stack of blades of various sizes along the back wall in the other abandon stalls. He was not surprised; Rowena had mentioned that her husband worked as a blacksmith. Stroking his hand down his long thick beard, Bram stood up and walked over to the barrel of water Lara had used to tend his wounds.

Needing to wash off the remaining dirt and dried blood, he dunked his head, shoulders and chest into the barrel until they were fully submerged in the water. The cool water offered some relief from the hot and humid summer night. Lifting out of the water, he tossed his long wet hair back over his shoulders. Drops of water cascaded down his beard and back, causing a prickling shiver down his spine. He then dipped his tunic into the water and rinsed off the blood and dirt though little would wash away. The stain had already begun to set in. Wringing the tunic out so that water was no longer dripping, he hung it over the wall of one of the stall doors to dry.

Snatching up one of the small blades and a whetstone which had been placed next to the stack, Bram carefully rubbed the stone along the blade's edge to sharpen it. Once he was satisfied the blade was good and sharp, he ran the blade down his face to remove the unwanted hair. Next, he cut his hair so that it hung no longer than his shoulders.

Once he finished, Bram placed the blade down onto the table and laid his weary body back down onto the pallet, hoping for a few hours of sleep before the sun rose. Closing his eyes, he allowed sleep to take him and he drifted off into a heavy slumber.

It felt like only an hour since Bram had fallen asleep when the sounds of the horses awakened him. He looked towards them wondering what had caused them to become so riled, as they stirred in their stalls. As he looked around the barn, he spied a wee lad, no more than seven or eight, who had entered and had been watching him as he slept. Taking a step back, the lad looked at him cautiously.

"Why do ye look like that?" the lad asked as he teetered back and forth along wooden beam.

"How do I look?" Bram smirked wondering which the lad referred to, his size or his scars.

"Like ye were attacked by wolves. I saw a wolf once. I was no' afraid of him though," the lad replied puffing out his chest as if he was showing off his muscles. Immediately he continued, "He was big like ye are. He killed one of our sheep. Would have killed another if it were no' fer my da. He bested him wit a shovel. Hit him over the head. If I'd had me a shovel, I would have hit him too," he proclaimed, swinging his arm back and forth as if he had some imaginary shovel in his hand. "By the way, me name is Tavish. What's yers?"

"Bram. Ye must be a brave warrior, Tavish," Bram chuckled giving the young lad a sense of pride.

"No' yet. But someday I will be a great warrior and I will kill all sorts of wolves. Are ye a warrior? Ye wear colors like one," he said eyeing Bram's kilt.

Bram looked down at his kilt. It no longer represented the brilliant colors of red and green that the MacKinnon Clan proudly wore but now displayed a dull hue of faded colors.

"I am," he admitted.

The lad smiled at him as if he was proud just to be in Bram's presence. *Attacked by wolves?* Bram chuckled at the lad's imaginative assumption. Even though that was not what had happened, the brutal treatment he'd received in the dungeon was comparable in nature to those of vicious wolves.

Just then an older man entered the barn. Tavish jumped down from the beam and ran past him back outside as if he would have been scolded for being there. Dressed in a stained tunic and dusty trews, the man raised a brow to Bram.

"Good day, Lad. My wife tells me ye are here to work for that pallet she had offered ye and the lass," the man said holding onto a small wooden bucket full of nails and a mallet.

"Aye," Bram replied reaching for his tunic, which had dried in the warm night air, and still hung over the stable wall. Donning his tunic, he stood up to greet the man properly.

"Good. Ye can start by helping me mend this roof. A storm like the devil's rage blew through here two nights ago; ripped it almost completely off. There are many planks that need replacing and I can no' do it myself. Me name is Innes and that wee hellion that just ran out like a windstorm was me son, Tavish."

"My name is Bram. And aye, yer son just introduced himself to me. For yer wife's gracious offer, I am glad to help ye."

Bram worked hard throughout the morning. He cut wood as instructed, of various shapes and sizes to fix the roof and the damaged fences. He then gathered bundles of reeds and thick straw, binding them together with rope and stacking each bundle high on top of wood beams erected to provide better shelter for the horses.

Sweat beaded across his forehead. Using the back of his hand, he wiped the sweat from his brow. The sun was high and not a cloud in the sky to offer him shade. Even if it had been a cooler or cloudier day, he would not be able to avoid the heat and his sore muscles.

"My last farmhand did no' work as hard as ye. Ye have me working to the bone and my body is in need of a break. Ye can stay here while I go fetch us some whisky. My mouth is as dry as the bark of a tree," Innes cracked a smile and climbed down the ladder.

Bram continued mending the roof until Innes returned with the two mugs of whiskey. Taking the mug from Innes, he held it in both hands, drinking slowly, savoring every drop. It was not the best whiskey he had ever had, but it tasted like sweet nectar in this moment. He did not remove the cup from his lips until he had swallowed every last drop of it.

As Bram and Innes returned to hammering the last few planks and beams on the roof, Innes spoke of his family, his work as a blacksmith, and the love he had for his wife. As for Bram, he mentioned little of himself.

Chapter 5

Lara awoke after the sun was already high in the sky. Sunlight filtered in through the open curtains like seams of gold. She could feel the daylight on her skin. Her eyes had not seen sunlight in weeks and they were stung by its brightness. Stretching out her arms, she rolled over her bed of blankets and sat upright.

Following a long-winded yawn, she wiped the sleep from her eyes and looked around the small living quarters. In the middle of the room stood a very tall and husky grey-haired man staring down at her with two mugs in his hands. Lara could feel her body stiffen with nervousness. Like a scared rabbit darting for cover, Lara grabbed onto the blanket and threw it over her shoulders like a shield hoping it would offer her some protection. Lara's eyes darted back and forth between the man and Rowena who was sitting down at a table kneading dough at the far end of the room, unaware of their interaction. Nervously, her grip on the blanket tightened.

"Good afternoon to ye, lass," the man cheerfully greeted.

"A...Afternoon?" Lara stuttered.

Lara knew that she had been completely exhausted but never would have dreamed that she would sleep so late in the day. Had they been watching her sleep? Lara could feel her cheeks heat and no doubt stain dark crimson in color.

The man smirked and let out a soft huff. Lara did not at all see the amusement in furthering her humiliation.

"Well my dearest wife, I will go check on the lad out in the barn while ye attend to the lassie," the man said as he kissed Rowena on the cheek and walked out the front door.

"That be my husband, Innes. Well now that ye are finally awake, why dinna ye tell me why ye are so far from home?" Rowena asked, as she continued flattening and rolling the ball of dough in her hands.

"How do ye ken I am far from my home?" Lara shakily asked, worried that Rowena had recognized her or perhaps knew that she had escaped from the English dungeon.

"Because ye are here and no' there," she replied, looking at Lara from underneath her long lashes.

Lara could see the suspicion in Rowena's eyes but pretended not to notice. As Lara stood up from the floor, she loosened the blanket around her, allowing it to drop to the floor. Rowena gasped.

"Good heavens child, what is that ye got on? Ye look like ye rolled around in the dirt wit' the pigs."

Lara rubbed her hands up and down her arms, not sure how to respond. She knew her appearance must look dreadful to the woman. The straps of her dress barely clung to her shoulders and the skirt was tattered. Her hair, which normally hung down in soft feathery layers was now disheveled, in knots, and coated in dirt.

Lara did not wish to lie to Rowena, but neither could she bring herself to tell the truth.

"I have been traveling for many days now and I lost my belongings along the way."

"Dinna ye worry lass, I may have a gown ye can wear," she said as she stood and walked over to Lara. "Follow me."

Lara gratefully followed her into the next room. The small chamber had a bed barely big enough for two and a small wooden chest. The walls were bare other than cobwebs and a year's worth of dust. In the corner, a roaring fire crackled in the fireplace. Murmuring to herself, Rowena dug through a pile of clothing and pulled out a brown wool dress and a white chemise.

"Ah, this will do. It is no' a fancy dress but anything is better than what ye got on," Rowena said as she laid it onto the bed. "I will go and fetch a few buckets of water I have heating so ye can wash."

Lara rejoiced over the thought of washing her face and hair. She could barely contain her excitement, but managed to keep a guarded and calm demeanor. Shortly after, Rowena came back into the room with two buckets of steaming water and emptied them into a shallow tub.

"Unless ye have further need of me, I will leave ye to wash."

"Nay, I need nothing else. Thank you, Rowena."

Lara began removing her once beautiful green gown and let it fall to the floor. It would now serve well as a rag. Anxiously, Lara dipped her feet into the hot water, one by one, and sank down into the tub. Lara looked down at the bruises that stained her body; reminders of what she had endured. She scrubbed herself thoroughly, hoping and wishing she could scrub them away, but the dark purple and blue marks remained. Unwanted tears escaped her eyes. She swore to herself that once she reached home no man would ever lay a hand on her again. As for her husband, her mind went through various scenarios as to how she would get her revenge, each one ending with him taking his last breath.

As soon as she had finished washing her hair, Lara donned the dress Rowena had left on the bed. It hung awkwardly off her shoulders; several sizes too large. Finding a ball of twine on the floor, Lara began to unravel it and wrapped it around her thin waist. Biting off one end at the perfect length, she tied the dress in place. She sat down next to the fire and used the towel to dry her hair. She was quick about it, anxious to leave.

Stepping back into the room, Rowena smiled.

"Oh, ye look verra fine lass, now that yer washed. The dress is a wee bit big but I am no' longer a young lass."

"It will do just fine. Thank ye," Lara replied, feeling renewed and refreshed.

"I best get a start on the day. When ye are done, come join me in the kitchen."

Lara nodded her head. She was grateful for Rowena's kindness, but would rather be on her way. *But to where?* She feared that if she returned home her father would send her back to her husband. If that happened, she was certain that Dermot would kill her, for he had no use for his defiant bride.

Lara knew that during the negotiations to unite their clans, Dermot had been furious that his father made the decision to unite the clans. After years of feuds, Dermot's hatred for the Fergussons was well known, and he protested the marriage. He was in love with another and insisted that he would deny his birthright as future Laird of Castle Foley if necessary to avoid marriage to Lara. But after he learned of the Fergusson clan's supposed "secret treasure", he became eager to marry Lara; too eager for her liking. His sudden change of heart disturbed her, but he had been a very persuasive suitor.

She still felt fury deep in the pit of her stomach for allowing Dermot to seduce her with words of passion and promises. He had given her hope for the future of her clan, and promised a good marriage. It was not until after their vows were spoken and before they even shared the marital bed, that he unmasked his true nature and motives.

He told her he had learned of a treasure, supposedly acquired by her father, and hoped to claim this treasure once they were married. Lara had never believed such treasure truly existed for no one had ever laid eyes upon it and only few knew of it. She recalled a moment when she was young, eavesdropping on her father, she'd heard about how he came to acquire it, but the details now were fuzzy. All Lara remembered hearing was that the treasure was a gift from a Norse King.

Lara did all she could to convince Dermot that it was merely a rumor and that no treasure existed. But her husband called her a liar and accused her of deceit. He began avoiding her, for which she was grateful. She despised him and fought him every time he tried to touch her. She would rather die a thousand deaths or be beaten beyond recognition before succumbing to him. He may have been her husband, but she refused to give him her maidenhood willingly.

Lara's mind wandered to a time when things were pleasant. When her mother, Elsa, was alive and her father was not the bitter man he became after Elsa's death. Since the day her mother passed, her father had seemed to care little for Lara's happiness and focused solely on her brother John. He'd pushed John into training longer and studying harder, obsessed with preparing John to one day be Laird of their clan. But grief alone did not explain her father's sudden change in behavior.

Lara shook her head, bringing her thoughts back to the present. Now was not the time to dwell on the past. She needed to think towards the future and how to expose Dermot for the treacherous man he was.

Lara stared into the flames. Her thoughts returned to the past day, then to Bram. She was anxious to see how he fared this day. Mayhap it was his kindness for helping her find shelter for the night, or perhaps it was because they shared an unspeakable bond as prisoners of war, but her thoughts lingered on him. She would at least thank him for his generosity.

Chapter 6

Once they had secured the last plank, Bram followed Innes down the ladder and headed towards the barn door to feed the horses. Grabbing onto an armful of hay, Bram carried it to the stalls. While the horses ate, he brushed their manes. The smaller of the two reminded him of a spirited young filly who was sired by his own horse. She was a beauty; light grey with white stockings. The mare restlessly kicked the back of her stall refusing to eat the fresh hay.

"Awe, dinna mind that one. She willnae eat while yer watching her. Free spirit that one is. Makes her untrainable and useless. I thought about selling her but I'd make better use of her using her hide as a covering to keep my arse warm," Innes joked.

Bram looked back to the fiery mare and smirked.

"I think ye have worked enough and are deserving of a fine meal," Innes exclaimed.

"Thank ye. I will join ye and yer gracious wife in a moment. I have still not yet finished wit the horses."

"Verra well," Innes said and walked back toward the house.

As Bram approached the black steed he had stolen, he was taken aback by what he discovered. Alongside the saddle bags were a broadsword and a pouch full of coin. Bram guessed that the men they had stolen the horse from were either wealthy travelers or a band of raiders who'd just filled their coffers. Either way, luck had been with him this day and the stars could not have aligned more perfectly. The cloak of ensuing darkness concealed the bags and Bram did not think to look about him as they were in dire need to escape quickly.

Strapping the small pouch to his belt, he headed towards the croft. His goal was to gather Lara and travel north to Dumfries. There, he could gather supplies for their journey to Lara's home and seek safe passage through the lowlands.

Lara quietly began slicing a loaf of bread while she listened to Rowena and Innes talking at the table. Mundane kitchen tasks were not something Lara was used to doing. At Stearns Castle, Lara was taught to weave and sew but nothing more. She never learned to read or write as it was against the church's teachings and forbidden by her father. It was her brother, John, who had taught her basic things such as how to use a dirk and wield a sword, even though Lara's thin arms could barely hold the weight of a sword over her head. But even her brother had been amazed by her way with a dagger.

John had been her only friend until he reached the age of ten and four and their father forced him to begin pursing his studies and training. She believed that his responsibilities to the clan became a heavy burden on him though he never shared his feelings towards it.

Lara's ears perked up when Innes mentioned Bram. She knew not why her heart quickened at the sound of his name or why she felt anxious to see him. But her curiosity got the better of her, causing her to lean towards them to get a better listen.

"The lad be doing a fine job this morning but something tells me that he is no' a farmhand," Innes said to his wife.

"Why do ye say that?" Rowena asked.

"Well, have ye seen the size of him? Built like a warhorse that one is," he replied.

"He said his name was MacKinnon. Have ye heard of them before?"

"Aye. I have heard of the MacKinnons from the north. But the lad is far from home if he be a MacKinnon. Reckless bunch, 'em Highlanders. They fight the English at every turn. And they dinna pay taxes like we have to. They fight fer their freedom while we cower behind it."

Innes's voice trailed off as he turned his head and looked out the window.

"Oh, Innes! We abide by the English rule and for that they spare us our lives and our land. That does no' mean that we have less pride than the Highlanders do, nor does it mean we are cowards. Ye are a good man and I will no' be hearing ye say any different," Rowena said in a frustrated tone. It seemed they'd had this conversation many times over.

Innes smiled back at Rowena in a loving gaze and placed his slightly wrinkled hand on her cheek. Lara could see the love the two of them shared. It was the kind of love she had hoped for in her own marriage, but instead she had married the Devil.

Lara heard the sound of gravel scuffling under heavy footsteps coming from outside the window and she headed towards the door. After a few taps on the door, Rowena stood and opened it. Filling the doorway stood a tall and roguish looking man. He wore a dull tan colored tunic slightly damp with sweat around the neckline. A faded red and green kilt hung over one shoulder and wrapped around his waist, held up by a brown leather belt. Lara could not draw her eyes from him. There was an overwhelming sense of familiarity about him. It took her several moments to realize that the man she was staring at was Bram. However, gone was the long mass of hair that had covered his face just yesterday. He was now clean shaven and his hair was much shorter, barely touching his shoulders.

Bram looked nothing like what she had imagined him to be. She had assumed he was older by the number of battle wounds on his body. Last eve he had not looked nearly as handsome as now. Lara was quite taken by him. There was something compelling yet daunting about him. He stood well over six feet tall and was more than twice her weight. Had she not observed his docile demeanor last night, she would have certainly been frightened of him. She smiled at the sight of him.

Bram's stomach rumbled with hunger when he smelled the scent of warm, freshly baked bread, as he walked closer to the croft. He would only stay for the meal and no longer. He had wasted enough time as it was. It was still too dangerous to be this close to the English border and he had no doubt that after the guards he had bested were discovered the English would send out a search party to find them.

He tapped on the door a few times but halted as the door flung open. Rowena greeted him with a wide smile and held her hand out to offer him entrance. The door frame hung so low that Bram had to slightly duck his head to enter. The room he entered was so small that it felt overcrowded. It was cluttered with tables and chairs, furs and fabrics, buckets and barrels. He wondered how anyone could move about in such chaos. He sat down on one of the chairs, fearful that his size would break it. Innes slid a mug of ale to him from across the table.

"It will take God Almighty himself to tear down that roof after all the hard work ye done to repair it," Innes said.

"Perhaps we should hire ye to be our farmhand permanently. Then maybe more of the work would get done around here. Dinna ken how many times I have asked Innes to fix that darn fence," Rowena jested.

"Now listen here, woman. I have told ye before. If ye wanted it done badly enough, ye could have done it. Then at least it would have been the way ye wanted it and I would no' be hearing any of yer complaining," Innes said as he playfully slammed Rowena's backside.

"Innes McDonald, ye have no' seen me complain yet," Rowena sarcastically replied and swatted his hand away.

"I love it when ye get angry," Innes said as his smile widened.

Both Innes and Rowena burst into laughter. Bram smirked at their playfulness. The way they acted reminded him of how his mother Kenna and father Duncan used to be before his father died. Since his death, he could not recall the last time his mother had a good hearty laugh. Lady Kenna gave up her duties as Lady of the castle. After giving up her primary responsibilities she took on the role of a healer and helped deliver bairns.

Rowena took a pitcher and refilled both Innes and Bram's mug before walking towards the corner of the room where she began filling a trencher with bread and a few slices of cheese. Bram wrapped his large hand around the handle and chugged its contents until he had finished it.

From the corner of his eye, he felt the sensation of being watched.

Bram took in a quick breath and held it as he looked over his shoulder. In the corner of the room stood a beautiful lass cutting a loaf of bread into small slices. It was Lara. Her hair was done up in braids, her pale face was rosy, and her lips were pink. She was a vision. Slowly, she came from behind the table with the trencher of bread in her hands.

"Good day," she said with a soft smile on her face.

When his eyes lit up, he could swear that her cheeks turned a brighter shade of red. As she moved closer, Bram watched every move, every curve. The sway of her hips was enticing even though the dress she wore did not flatter her slim figure. It was dull and shapeless and had a cord of twine tied around her thin waist. As she came closer, Bram could see every feature of her face. From her small pointed nose to her sterling grey eyes. She was a natural beauty. He wanted to hit himself over the head for not noticing earlier how bonnie the lass was. She leaned in and placed the tray onto the table between him and Innes.

Nodding his head to her, he uttered, "Good afternoon. If I may say so, ye look like a lady!"

Her eyes widened by his failed attempt at a compliment. Giving her a sideways smile, he felt like a complete idiot.

"Was I no' a lady before I bathed?" she replied raising an eyebrow.

Innes snickered. Bram could hear the sarcasm in her tone. Her words pricked him like the tip of a dirk. If he had insulted her, it was of his own doing; never had the beauty of a woman riled him so. He fumbled his words and could not think clearly enough to reconcile his attempt at a compliment. . He had only been thinking with his cock.

"Of course ye are a lady. That's no' what I meant. I meant to compliment ye. Ye are a…," Bram searched for the right words to say, "comely lass."

Lara brushed her hands down the front of her skirt her expression indicated she was about to reply when Tavish entered the croft.

"Mum, Da, I think the wolf is back. I am goin' to set up a trap and get him this time!" he said as he held up a fist full of feathers.

"Brave lad," Rowena said and held him in a motherly embrace. "Ach, laddie, ye are getting so big. Before I ken it, I will nay be able to wrap my arms around ye."

Tavish smiled. He regaled them with the story of his adventures and coming upon the feathers, trying hard not to leave out any detail.

"One day, I will be a big and strong warrior like Bram," he said pointing in Bram's direction.

"A warrior, ye say?" Rowena repeated.

"Aye, he told me."

Bram could feel the eyes of everyone in the room upon him. But it was their silence that made him uncomfortable. Thankfully, Tavish had quickly redirected their attention once more.

"The wench is awake!" Tavish exclaimed, pointing at Lara.

"Tavish!" Rowena barked and scowled deeply at him, horrified by what her son had just said.

"But da said…" Tavish tried to explain.

Lara's face turned crimson with embarrassment. Did these people think she was a whore - or worse, *his* whore, she thought, as she looked at Bram in utter dismay.

"Never mind what yer da said," Rowena growled giving both him and Innes a cautioning look.

"Da, are we still going to the market at Dumfries? Ye promised to take me wit' ye today," Tavish asked before his mother scalped him.

"I would, laddie, but there is much to be done 'round here. I will take ye next time."

"Is Dumfries a great distance from here?" Bram asked.

"Nay. Only a few hours north and west from here," Innes replied.

"Thank ye again fer the food and fer allowing us to stay, but I am afraid we must be off. Lara, would you care to join me outside?"

Lara nodded and followed him out the door.

"My lady, we will be traveling to Dumfries. It should be on the way to yer home. I am friends with the Laird of Montrose just west of town. He can offer us supplies and safe passage through the Lowlands against the Campbells. My clan is nay an ally wit' the Campbells and if we were to travel around their land it would take several days."

"Must we stop? I am friends with the Campbells. Surely they would no' attack if I am wit' ye."

"Aye, that may be true lass, but that dinna mean that they will nay try to kill me. I made a promise that ye will arrive safe at Stearns Castle, so I must do what is necessary. I can no' promise ye that the journey will be wi'out danger. These southern hills are steep and dangerous to travel, and I dinna take too kindly to the southern clans. Many of 'em are in support of the English."

"I can hold my own. I am no' afraid," she said.

Lara wondered if going to Dumfries, or Montrose for that matter, was a good idea. She needed to get home as soon as she could to explain to her father what had happened. This detour would only delay her and she could not afford to waste another day for fear that Dermot would find she had escaped. But she knew that Bram was right. If they were to make this journey, and if he were to continue on to the Highlands, he would need supplies.

"Best ye say yer goodbyes."

Lara could hear the severity in his tone and did not wish to make him wait any longer. Nodding her head, she turned to say her goodbye to Rowena thanking her for her hospitality and apologizing for her abruptness in leaving.

"Will I ever see ye again?" Tavish asked Bram.

"I dinna ken Tavish, but I hope to see ye again someday. I may have use of a strong warrior," he smiled fondly at him.

Lara followed Bram to the stables. Using a stool, she mounted the horse and waited for Bram to do the same.

Chapter 7

With lightning speed they raced over the hills, passing vast fields and meadows, until they entered a dense forest and were forced to slow their pace. The sunlight shone through the branches of the canopy, and a pungent, earthy smell of morning dew hung in the air.

"My lady, we will take a short rest up ahead."

Bram slowed the horse, stopping along a shaded glade.

"I will need a moment of privacy as well," she told him.

"Aye, but dinna be too long. I am no' certain whose land this may be, and whether they are friend or foe."

Bram helped Lara dismount. She followed the sound of trickling water that led to a nearby creek. The water seeped down a winding path and emptied into a small pond. The foliage was thick and lush. Lara welcomed the shade that offered her protection against the scorching sun. Leaning towards the water, she dipped her hands in the stream to cool her face.

She returned shortly after to find Bram tightening the straps on the horse.

"Are ye hungry?" he asked her.

"Aye. I have no' eaten since this morning and then I ate only a little."

Bram opened the flap of the saddle bag and pulled out a smaller brown bag and handed it to Lara. Inside was an apple and some dried venison.

"The men we borrowed the horse from were kind enough to stock the saddle bags with food and coin," he noted, as his lips turned up at the corners.

Lara had almost forgotten that they had stolen the beautiful black steed. She was grateful they had found the horse when they needed it, and prayed their good fortune would continue.

"If ye are ready, we should be on our way. I want to make it to Dumfries before the sun sets," Bram suggested, interrupting her thoughts.

Lara cringed at the thought of being back in the saddle. Her aching muscles were one thing, not to mention the strange sensations caused by being held in Bram's arms. She tried to sit as upright as possible, keeping her distance, but he scooted closer to her, holding on to her even tighter. She hoped it was just to make sure she was secure on the horse, and nothing more.

When they finally reached Dumfries, the hour was late. Lara's thighs and bottom burned from the hours spent in the saddle and she felt exhausted.

"May I help ye down, lass?" Bram asked, holding his arms up to her.

Lara smiled down at him for his chivalry. She swung her leg over the saddle and took him by the hand as she slid down the side of the horse.

"Thank ye," she said and curtsied.

But when she took a step, her knees buckled, and she collapsed to the ground. Sitting for so long on the saddle had caused her legs to go weak and turned her backside numb.

"Are ye alright, lass?" Bram asked, kneeling down beside her.

"Aye," she responded with a crooked smile, and allowed Bram to help her back to her feet.

With Lara in his arms, Bram could not help noticing how weightless she felt even wearing the baggy wool dress. There was no doubt he was besotted with her, but she was no wench. This close, he could smell the lavender in her hair and the softness of her skin as he cradled her in his arms. As he held her, his manhood grew, but he desperately tried to ignore it.

Once she was steady on her feet, he released her but her body remained close to his. He wanted to think that she felt comfort there, but just as he thought it, she stepped back. He searched her eyes, looking to see if she shared his desire, but they looked tired, with dark circles shadowing the lower lids.

"Thank ye," she said, holding his gaze.

"Yer welcome."

Along the thoroughfare were several shops and merchant stalls filled with food, fabrics and pottery. The town was bustling with shoppers purchasing their goods.

As they browsed the stalls of merchants, a woman stepped out in front of Bram. Wearing a tightly fitted red gown with a low neckline, she quickly caught his attention. The woman gave him a mischievous smile but when she looked at Lara her smile faded.

"That be a fine medallion you wear around your neck. Ye can fetch a mighty price for that piece of silver," the woman said in a thick French accent, eyeing the medallion that hung low around Bram's neck.

He had kept it secured in the lining of his kilt while imprisoned so that the guards knew not who he was or to which clan he belonged. But now, free from danger, he wore it proudly.

"Aye, and what would ye offer fer it?" Bram asked, curious to know what worth it had to the woman.

"If it is coin you seek I can offer you plenty, or maybe the company of a warm bed for a prize piece like that one," the woman responded, placing a finger on his forearm, slowly drawing it up and down. Displaying a devilish smile, she continued, "A trade, perhaps?"

Bram met her gaze. Her regard showed that she was quite persistent. He stepped closer so that he was out of earshot of Lara.

"What sort of a trade?" he curiously asked.

Bram's instinct told him not to trust the woman but his curiosity got the better of him. And he had to admit that under normal circumstances, the voluptuous woman was exactly the type who often warmed his bed.

Squeezing his upper arm, she pulled him closer. She had the sweet smell of lilac and Bram could not stop his eyes from tracing down her neckline and dwelling on her well-exposed bosom. She stepped up on her toes so that her head was near his. He could feel her breath against his ear.

She whispered, "Information."

Information? He pondered. What sort of information would this harlot have that he could possibly want? Or need?

"What use would that do me?" he asked. "I have nay need for useless words, woman. But for a price I would be willing to sell ye the medallion."

The woman squinted as if she struggled with her choices. Taking a deep breath, she puffed it all out at once and nodded.

"Well, as I am feeling most generous today, I shall give you both," she said.

Shifting to his side and wrapping her arm around his, the woman directed him away from the crowd and between two of the shops. Slowly, the woman spoke, articulating each word as if she needed to choose them carefully. Her eyes fixed on Lara.

"You are in grave danger with that chit accompanying you."

"What sort of danger?"

"If she is the lass I believe her to be, there were men here in the village searching for her. But

I can say no more. I do not know who they were. These walls are thin and ears are everywhere. You must take her and be gone from this place."

Bram did not know whether or not to believe her allegations. The little information she gave him caused his mind to race with a hundred unanswered questions. Bram silently removed his medallion and handed it over to the woman. It made no difference to him if the woman had this medallion or not; he had two others at home.

The woman snatched it greedily and pulled out a small leather pouch kept in the bosom of her dress. Handing the bag to Bram, she turned and quickly made her way down the passageway until the darkness swallowed her whole.

"Is something wrong?" Lara asked.

"Nay lass, the woman was just talking nonsense," he replied. He thought it best to keep what the woman had said to himself, for now. But first, he needed Lara to tell him exactly who she was and why the English had imprisoned her.

Chapter 8

At the end of the market square, Bram spotted a tavern tucked away far from the fray where they could have a meal without attracting unwanted attention. Entering through the door, the tavern was lively - full of music and energy. The booming sound of men's laughter could be heard echoing off the stone walls, while drunken dancers twirled around, their ale splashing out of their mugs and onto the floor. There was not a single table or chair that was not occupied. Bram took out a few coins from his pouch.

Slipping the coins into Lara's hand, he whispered, "Stay here and dinna go anywhere.

"Where are ye going?" Lara asked loudly over the noise of the crowd.

Bram could sense her worry. But his instinct told him that it was best to not bring her to Montrose keep. If Lara was in some sort of danger, he did not know what to expect from Stephen.

"I am off to Montrose. I will no' be long. I think it is best if I go alone. I have no' seen Laird Stephen in many years' time and I dinna ken where his allegiance lies. I may no' be able to protect ye while I am there. It is best that ye stay here and wait fer my return."

Even though Bram was unsure whether he should leave Lara here, he wanted to take the warning he'd received in the market seriously. He knew that at least one greedy person knew her whereabouts and who she might be. He did not want to take the chance of more people discovering until he knew the complete situation.

"I thought ye said that he was a friend. Can ye no' trust him?"

"Aye, he has been a good friend, but he would stick a knife in yer back to save his own arse if given the choice."

"What shall I do, if the English come, or if I need to find ye?" Lara asked in a trembling voice.

"Dinna worry lass. Just stay here within the market. Dinna venture off too far and ye will be fine. I have given ye enough coin if ye want to buy something in the market. I will be back soon," he said as he began to turn towards the door. Just as he turned, he looked back at her and said, "And lass, when I return there are some questions that are in need of answering. I can no' help ye if ye are keeping secrets from me."

Without allowing her the time to explain or ask him to what he referred, Bram walked away. Like a startled deer, Lara froze. She fidgeted with her hands as she wondered what secrets he could have been talking about. She stood with her mouth agape, but it was as if he'd taken her voice with him. She had hoped that he would just escort her to Fergusson land without questions. She wrung her hands together, dreading their next encounter.

Bram followed the river several miles south until he reached the gates of Montrose Castle. With the sun well below the horizon, the murky water within the castle's moat looked ominous. The night air was darkened by a veil of heavy cloud that hovered between him and his final destination. Bram dismounted, strapping his sword to his side. As Bram approached the castle, he could see light flickering from a dim lantern at the top of the tower and guards pacing back and forth between the turrets.

"State yer business or be gone wit' ye," a guard called out from a small door of the gatehouse.

"My name is Bram MacKinnon. I wish to have an audience with the Laird of this keep."

"Our Laird does no' wish to see any visitors today. Come back tomorrow and ye can make yer request then."

"I'm afraid that tomorrow may be too late. It is of great importance that I see him. If ye will only give him my name," Bram continued but the guard quickly interrupted.

"Yer name is of nay importance. It is the dead of night and we have our orders. None shall pass these gates without prior notice."

"I have visited here before. Montrose used to be friendly and welcomed travelers. Is there a reason why it is nay that way any longer?"

"Aye. But I dinna see why I need to tell ye about it," The guard replied and turned up his mouse-like nose.

As silence passed between them, Bram grew more impatient with the guard. He knew that he needed to press the guard harder into opening the gates for him. Laird Stephen was the only man in the lowlands that held a high enough position to offer him the services he needed. Bram knew that without supplies, he would never be able to journey all the way to the Highlands before winter weather came upon him.

"If ye refuse to allow me entrance ye can be certain that the English will be the ones barging in these gates, for they may only be a few days ride from here."

The guard looked at him strangely. His voice changed from a loud growl to a sullen tone as he acknowledged the urgency of the situation.

"I will summon our Laird. Remove yer weapons and I will open the gate."

Bram did as he was asked and handed his sword to the guard. He followed him to the entrance of the keep and was asked to wait in the bailey while the guard went inside to convey his message.

In the bailey, several guards kept watch at their posts. The atmosphere felt strange. This was not the Montrose Castle Bram remembered. Then again, it had been years since he stepped foot inside the castle walls. The bailey, formerly full of activity with peasants and warriors alike, was now barren except for two masons who were repairing a section of the wall that had been badly damaged. Bram now understood the reason for the increased security and the guard's hesitation.

Behind him, a familiar voice called out his name, "Bram MacKinnon! I can no' believe me eyes. I heard that ye were killed in battle. But here ye are."

"Did ye really believe the English could have bested me? Ye should ken never to underestimate a MacKinnon," Bram responded, smiling back at the man. "It is good to see ye, Max."

Shaking the man's hand, Bram said, "And ye as well. What happened here?"

"Ah, our castle was attacked by the English. Many of my men died in battle. It took us a good month or two to rid our lands of the English. But tell me, why have ye made such a long journey to my keep? Did yer brother send ye?"

"Nay. My brother dinna ken I survived. He must think me dead and rotting in the ground. Nay, I have come to ask ye fer yer help. I need safe passage back to the Highlands but first I must travel through the black forest towards Fergusson lands."

Bram watched as the skin between Stephen's eyebrows furrowed.

"Fergusson? Why would ye go so far west? And to that bastard's land?" Stephen growled.

"I am traveling wit' a lass. I have vowed to protect her and see her safely home to her family."

"I am no' allied wit' the Fergussons and neither are ye. That bastard is the English King's vassal. Why would ye want to help a Fergusson lass? Did prison turn ye into an eejit?"

"I ken they are not allies. But she saved my life. She dinna ken that our clans feud. She kens nothing of politics and nay about who their enemies are."

"Well, she must be a clever lass fer ye to be so trustin' of her. Either that or she is daft."

"I made a promise, Stephen. I am no' going to break it."

Stephen's eyes narrowed, "She must mean a great deal to ye for ye to risk traveling through the black forest and Fergusson land."

Bram glared at him for his suggestion. The man thought to insult him and Lara. He would not stand there and let Lara's honor be questioned. If he had to, he would toss Stephen on his arse until he minded his tongue.

In a deep growl, he replied, "As I said, I owe her my life and fer that, I am helping the lass. That is all."

"I dinna mean any disrespect. If ye need safe passage I can have me men send a message to the Campbells on yer behalf. Take what supplies ye need," Stephen offered. "We have been friends a long time, Bram, and I will help ye, but if it comes to war, I will no' be a part of it."

Bram nodded. "I thank ye fer yer hospitality. When I return home, I will make sure my brother pays ye in kind."

Stephen gave him a grim look before responding.

"Take the road to the west and then north through the woods. The English troops have been spotted to the west. Ye should nay have any trouble if ye keep off the road."

"Thank ye."

Stephen bid him farewell and walked back inside the keep. Bram turned and headed in the opposite direction towards the casemate. There he found weapons, armor and a few logs of peat. Marg, one of the servants, came in and gave him extra clothing, a blanket, and food. Once he'd stored the supplies in the saddle bags, he left to head back to Dumfries.

Lara swirled the remaining wine in her cup before taking another sip. The taste of cloves and nutmeg lingered on her lips. It reminded her of her mother, Elsa. Elsa drank heavily and favored the wine. As much as Lara carried with her fond memories of her mother, she only remembered her mother's unexplained sadness towards the end. She was a woman who could never be pleased, and would always fight and argue with Lara's father, though Lara never knew why. On the night she passed, she had summoned Lara to her bed chamber. She spoke of mishaps and regrets but Lara did not understand any of it and by the time the fever came she was talking nonsense. Lara forced her thoughts back to the present, finished her cup of mulled wine, and returned to the market.

As she made her way through the carts of beautiful fabrics, she ran her hand across the rolls of silk and lace. Lara had missed the gowns and riding dresses she was forced to leave behind at Castle Foley when she fled. She was grateful that Rowena had given her a gown to wear, as her gown had been so badly damaged. But she couldn't help thinking to herself that the wool fabric made her sweat more than a farmer working in the blistering sun.

As she admired the linen and lace, Lara saw from the corner of her eye someone following her. It was the woman who Bram had spoken to earlier. Her conspicuous behavior made it hard for Lara to ignore. Slowly, the woman approached.

"Good day to you, my lady. Tis good fortune that our paths have crossed. I know what is in your future," the woman said.

The woman spoke with a French accent. Lara eyed her curiously.

"My future? And how do ye ken of such things?" Lara asked.

"Follow me into my tent and I can show you," she said grabbing onto Lara's upper arm and escorting her into a large tent with dark red linen walls.

"Ye are nay a merchant?" Lara asked as she vividly recalled her standing next to one of the carts in the market.

"Of sorts," the woman replied.

Inside the tent was a small round table with two chairs sitting opposite each other. In the middle of the table were small stones with bizarre markings and a small stack of thick pieces of paper with painted pictures of exotic and unusual designs. Lara was hesitant for a moment but accepted the chair when the woman offered for her to sit.

"Ye are a gypsy!" Lara exclaimed, her voice louder than it had been before.

The woman laughed at Lara's reaction.

"I am a woman of many talents. Telling futures is just one of them."

Lara squinted her eyes in skepticism and waited for the woman to speak. She was curious as to how the woman would perform such a task, for no one, even Lara, could not know her future. She decided that this sort of activity was made for a good jest or wishful thinking but did not for a fleeting moment believe that this woman could predict the future.

Patiently, she sat and waited. The woman grasped the stack of paper and pulled out three pieces at random. The first card was flipped over, showing a picture of a man who looked as if he was in pain. He slumped over to one side and his face had a saddened look upon it.

"I see death. But this death is not in the future, but in the past."

Lara swallowed hard. She did not know the meaning behind what the woman said. The only person who had died was her mother, but the woman could not have known that. However, it could have been said about anyone as the statement was vague and she did not mention to whom she referred. Lara continued to watch and listen.

Her eyes followed the woman's hand as she flipped over the next one. The painting depicted a picture of a jeweled golden cup similar to one she imagined would be used for royalty. The drawing itself, Lara thought, was drawn by a very talented artist.

"You are searching for something. No' a place, or a person. A treasure mayhap?" she said in a gravelly tone.

Lara took her eyes off the painted card and popped her head up. Suddenly, this fortune-telling was becoming all too real for her.

Shaking her head in disbelief, she murmured, "How can ye ken that?"

"I can only tell you what the cards say. I cannot explain why."

"How can ye or yer cards ken that?"

"If my cards say tis real, than tis real," the woman barked. "Perhaps it is not for you to find the treasure."

Abruptly pushing herself from the chair, Lara stood. She was no longer going to subject herself to this woman's insanity. She had learned nothing by this encounter and all it had done was aggravate her. She wished that she had never agreed to enter the tent with this foolish woman. And this experience was far from entertaining.

The woman had said things, things she could not have known. Lara felt that her first instinct was correct; the woman was nothing more than a fraud with a silver tongue.

Noticing Lara had become upset, the woman said, "I can only tell you what the cards say, my lady. But I can tell you this. That whatever answers you are searching for will only lead you into danger. In truth, I know who you are, and I know that you are in more danger than you think."

"Danger! From whom? How do ye ken me?"

"You are in danger from the men sent to find you. A group of them passed through here just last night. I do not know who they are, but they were to make certain that you do not return."

"What makes ye think they search fer me?"

"Because, ye are Lady Moray, are ye not? Though their description of you does not do you justice."

After a few silent moments between them, Lara turned and walked out of the tent and back into the sea of shoppers. After walking only a few steps, she became dizzy. Her stomach twisted in knots and she could not stop her hands from shaking. *Dermot*, she thought. Had he found out she'd escaped the English, he would have indeed sent men out to search for her.

She looked around at the faces of the people passing by to see if she recognized any of them. Once her stomach settled enough for her to walk, she quickly made her way back to the tavern to wait for Bram.

Chapter 9

Bram returned to Dumfries just as people were beginning to close their shops and pack away the items stacked on the carts. He walked past a stall that had a variety of colored silk and linen dresses and other women's wear. His thoughts turned to Lara and the oversized wool dress she had been wearing. The wool dress, he thought, must be hot and uncomfortable for her, though she had not complained once.

Interrupting a seamstress packing away her wares, he inquired about the cost of a dark blue gown that caught his eye. He thought the rich color would look beautiful on Lara with her dark hair. Not that he had much of a fashion sense about such things, but blue was his favorite color. He couldn't deny his impulse to see Lara covered in such a fine fabric.

While he was there, he also thought to buy her a pair of boots. Traveling barefoot, especially in the woods, was never a good idea, even if one's feet were as calloused as his. He imagined her feet to be small and delicate. Unsure of Lara's size, he useds the seamstress' size as a reference. It was a good thing that the woman was not plump, otherwise he would not have known how to describe the lass without insulting this one. Once he'd paid for the items and placed them in the saddle bags, he rode towards the tavern hoping to find Lara unharmed.

He found Lara inside the tavern at the far end of the room, sitting at a table surrounded by men. His hand went right to the hilt of his sword and he marched towards them. Listening to the drunken fools, he could tell they openly flirted with her. They asked to buy her drinks, or share a dance.

"Nay, thank ye. I am waiting here fer someone," she said to them as they huddled around her.

"Ah, come on lassie. Just one wee dance. 'Tis all I'm asking," one of the men said, placing his hand upon her shoulder.

"Best ye remove yer hand Sir, if ye favor it," Lara snapped and scooted away.

Bram grinned when he heard her sharp tongue but the fact that they were still trying to pursue her did not sit well with him. If anyone was going to pursue the lass, it was going to be him. He would not idly stand there and allow any other man the opportunity. If the need arose, he would fight off every one of these bastards, throw her over his shoulder, and walk out the door.

"I believe the lass said nay to yer advances," Bram growled.

Four of the men that surrounded Lara turned their heads in his direction. Three of them were smaller than Bram and looked as if they were about to piss their trews. The fourth, however, was similar to Bram in size, and did not take Bram's interruption too kindly. The man crossed his arms over his chest and stood in front of Lara; blocking her from Bram's view.

"And who are ye to say that the lass willnae change her mind?"

"I am her escort," Bram replied, trying to keep calm.

Clutching his free hand into a tight fist, Bram's anger rose, and this man added fuel to the fire. The other men took a step back.

"Well, it seems she has a new escort now," the man declared.

Chuckling, the man turned his attention back to Lara. With one foot up on a chair and the other planted on the ground, he leaned towards her. Bram could feel the heat of his anger rising. It was a force to be reckoned with. Like a wild beast protecting its young, Bram swung his fist and punched the man hard on the side of his head, causing him to flip over the table and go tumbling to the ground. Bram stood over him, waiting for the man to get up and continue to brawl, but the man did not move. His head lolled to the side, his eyes remained closed, and spittle dripped from the left corner of his mouth. Bram had knocked him out cold. As for the other three, Bram watched as they cowered, then took off running out the door. As mad as a raging storm, Bram stomped back to where Lara was still sitting at the table. She looked affright, but something inside of him knew that it wasn't the men that frightened her, it was him.

In a brash voice, he uttered, "It is time to go, lass."

As they walked out the door, Bram said nothing to her. He knew that she must have thought his actions were harsh and uncalled for, but he had good reason. It had driven him mad seeing those men huddled around her; flirting and making advances. He justified what he had done by his promise to protect her, but he knew that he would only be fooling himself.

"Thank ye," she whispered.

Her low and sweet voice carried on the wind behind him and he could barely make out her words.

"Yer welcome."

"Ye dinna have to do that. I was able to handle myself just fine. They were being proper gentlemen."

"Ye shouldnae be so trusting," he barked, not meaning to sound so harsh.

"Are ye saying that I welcomed their attention?" she quickly interjected.

Bram could hear the anger in her voice.

"Nay," he replied and paused for a moment. "Men like them cannae be trusted. I dinna mean to frighten ye nor am I mad at ye. I am only mad at myself. Had I been there ye would nay have been in that situation. I promised I would protect ye and I meant it."

The light in Lara's eyes softened. Bram had to muster all his strength not to grab her, pull her into his arms, and press his lips to hers in a hard and passionate kiss. The force he felt between them was as strong as the tides. He did not know what stopped him from trying except for the fact that most lasses he took to his bed were not lairds' daughters.

Wanting to forget this whole bloody thing, Lara asked, "Will we be traveling tonight by horse?"

He waited to catch up with her before he replied, "Nay, lass. Tis too late to travel tonight. We will get a room at the inn and leave by first light."

His voice sounded much calmer than it had earlier and for that Lara was grateful. She did not wish to argue with him nor did she want to be in his company if he continued to stay angry.

Lara waited outside of the inn while Bram made arrangements to obtain a room for the night. He walked out the door moments later with a key in hand.

The room was small, with barely enough room to walk around the bed, let alone sleep on the floor. When Bram stated they would sleep in the room together, Lara wanted to protest, but she remained silent. How could she claim that it was not proper for a married woman to sleep in the same room as another man, when in fact she already had? In the dungeon, she was surrounded by men and not one of them was her husband. Her stomach felt like it was twisted in knots as she struggled with the morality of the situation.

While Bram started a fire in the hearth, he insisted that she sleep on the bed and he would lay upon the floor, but the thought of taking such luxury for herself at his expense was unthinkable. She did not deserve to be lounging in comfort while Bram, who was still wounded from his beatings, lay on the hard floor without a pallet, or even a blanket. There were only enough bed coverings for one.

"Lass, I am used to sleeping on the ground. Now, dinna argue wit' me."

Lara suppressed a smile.

"Ye say that a lot, ye ken. Mayhap I enjoy a good argument now and then," Lara jested, hoping to lighten the mood.

Bram smiled and shook his head. Before she knew it, they both started laughing.

"Well, then I promise ye that ye can argue wit' me anytime, but I must warn ye that I can be quite stubborn and dinna give way too easily. No' even fer a bonny lass."

Lara blushed. No man had ever called her bonny before. She did not believe that he really meant what he said and assumed that it was just his way of making peace after he had been so angry earlier.

Lara fought hard to hold back her yawns. She was tired after spending her day in the market walking around the different shops. She made her way to the bed.

Distracted by his anger at the men in the tavern, Bram had forgotten the gifts in the saddle bags. He thought that now would be an appropriate time to give them to her. Excusing himself, he hurried outside to the horse and pulled out the parcel that contained the gown and boots.

Returning to the room, Bram laid the package, tied with twine, on the bed before her.

"I almost forgot. I bought you something."

"A gift?"

"Nay. A necessity."

Lara opened the bag and pulled out a blue gown and a pair of leather boots. Tears came to her eyes.

"Bram, they are lovely. But ye really shouldnae have."

"Lass, ye needed the boots. And the wool dress ye were wearing is too hot fer this heat. The thinner material should offer ye more comfort."

"Thank ye," she said as she stood up and held up the dress against her.

The silk gown was the deep blue of sapphires, and tiny pearls were sewn along the neckline. The sleeves were short and the skirt flowed down beyond her toes. Bram inwardly smiled at the cheerful expression Lara wore as she folded the dress and placed it over the back of a chair before settling back into bed. He watched as her eyes slowly closed in slumber.

Finding a spot on the floor, Bram lay down on the ground and went to sleep.

Lara awoke to the sound of Bram moaning. Rolling over to the edge of the bed, she looked down at him on the floor. She watched as he tossed and turned as if he were struggling to break free from some imaginary hold. Sitting up in the bed, she scooted herself to the edge and stood. Quietly, she walked over to him. Kneeling down next to him she watched him as his eyes rapidly rolled back and forth under their lids and his head tossed side to side. His forehead glistened with sweat.

Afraid to touch him, she whispered, "Bram."

There was no answer. Calling him a second time still did not wake him. Lara held her hand up, wanting to touch his shoulder, but hesitated and withdrew her hand. She waited several long moments before slowly bringing it down. With a gentle stroke of her hand, she caressed his shoulder. His skin was hot to the touch but as soft as a bairn's bottom.

She had never touched a man besides her husband. Dermot was not as big or strong as Bram was. His shoulders and arms were not as sculpted with muscle and he did not have the musky smell of horse and leather. Dermot was very different from Bram. He was cruel and selfish; two things that Bram could never be. Bram was honest, honorable, and risking his life for her, though he knew nothing of her past. Had he taken the horse, he would be half way home by now, she thought. She could not bear the guilt she felt at keeping him away from his family. In the morning, she would insist that he allow her to ride home alone.

Lara, realizing she had been admiring him for longer than what seemed appropriate, quickly tapped him on the shoulder.

Bram's eyes popped open at her touch and in one swift movement, he had her pinned beneath him, holding her wrists high above her head.

Lara's breathing quickened and she began to shake vigorously. She had no idea what had happened or what Bram was about to do. The hazy look in his eyes told her that he was furious and she began to regret waking him from his dream.

"Bram… Bram, ye are hurting me," she said.

His weight pressed down against hers such that she could barely breathe.

Bram released her wrists and sat up. The angry look on his face changed quickly at the sight of her.

"Why did ye wake me? Dinna ye ken that ye should never wake a sleeping man? I could have killed ye," he grumbled, and scowled at her.

"I dinna mean to anger ye. But ye were tossing and turning, and I..." she tried to explain before getting choked up.

"I am sorry lass. I dinna mean to frighten or hurt ye," Bram said as he leaned in towards her to wipe a tear from her cheek.

"What were ye dreaming about?" she stammered in between sharp inhalations.

"I was dreaming of battle. Over the last sennight, it has kept replaying in my mind."

Lara creased her brow and frowned. She never realized a man like him could be haunted so fiercely by battle.

"I'm sorry," she repeated hoping to make amends.

"Lass, why did the English have ye? The truth now. Who was it that gave ye over to the English?" he questioned, needing to know the answer so he knew how to protect her and from whom.

"My husband, Laird Dermot Moray," she said in such a faint whisper that he was certain he misunderstood her.

"Yer husband? Ye are married?" he asked in surprise, losing his breath for a moment.

"Aye. I was sold to the English to pay my husband's taxes to the King."

Married? Bram felt as if an arrow had plunged deep into his heart. What kind of a father would marry his daughter off to such a whoreson? And what kind of husband would treat his wife in such a cruel manner?

"Why would yer husband do such a thing, lass?"

Lara bit her bottom lip. She was agitated and uncertain whether she wanted to share her story with him. But he had been kind towards her, and she believed she could trust him. She took a deep breath, and started from the beginning.

"I was sent to live at Castle Foley just north of Irvine. My father felt that Laird Moray was a good military man with power, money, and the English King's ear."

Lara quickly clarified when she saw Bram's look of betrayal.

"Tis no' what ye think. We are no' traitors. Most of the Lowland clans live under the English King's rule, but our allegiance is still to Scotland," she explained, releasing the breath that she had been holding. "At first I did no' want to marry him. I was scared of him, but when he learned of our betrothal, he… he," she stuttered.

Lara tried to find the right words to say. In truth, at the beginning of their courtship he was kind and it was only after their wedding that he became the monster she now knew him to be.

"He was benevolent," she continued saying. She did not dare refer to him as kind.

"After our wedding ceremony, all of his friendliness changed. There is a rumor that my dowry holds a rare treasure but no one has ever laid eyes upon it. It was said that it was given to my father from a Norse King. But my father remains silent about it and will no' say whether the claim is true, nor prove it to be false. The only thing he would admit was that he had once held a high command with the Norse King's army before he married my mother."

"And I take it that Laird Dermot found out about this treasure?" Bram asked.

"Aye. Which is why he agreed to the union. When I swore to him that I knew nothing of it, he called me a liar. He kept insisting that my father and I kept it hidden. But I showed him our treasure room, the secret passageways, and the trunks locked in the sacristy, but he still did no' believe me. He demonstrated a false impression of wealth to the neighboring clans but when the English came to collect the taxes, Dermot had no money to pay them. He gave the English me instead of coin. He ne'er wanted the union, he told me. He said I was plain and useless as a wife, and that he wished he had ne'er married me. That is why I must go home."

"What of yer father? Surely if he knew the truth, he would strike the bastard down and protect ye from harm."

"Nay. I told my father how Dermot treated me, but he said that I needed to be a dutiful wife and obey my husband."

"Lass, I make a promise to ye that nay any more harm will come to ye. I will take ye to yer father, but if yer father will no' help ye, ye can come wit' me to Dunakin. Ye would be welcomed there."

"Thank ye, but ye dinna have to, Bram. Ye have done more than enough. Ye have been away from yer family long enough and I will no' keep ye from them any longer."

"Aye, it has been a while, but I can wait a little longer. Dinna argue wit' me, lass; I will no' be changing my mind."

By the time she had finished her tale, her eyes were reddened from tears. Bram wore a deep frown and knew not what to say. He felt sorry for the lass and the way she was treated, and she was anything but plain and useless. She was beautiful, and from what little he knew of her, she was resilient and courageous. Had she nowhere to go, Bram would gladly offer her a place within his clan. He knew that his brother would take her in and that all of his clansmen would show nothing but kindness. He could only hope that her father would offer her the compassion and protection that she deserved.

Chapter 10

The night passed quickly. When morning was upon them, Bram crept out of the room to allow Lara to continue resting before their long journey. Once he had prepared the horse, he went back to the room to wake Lara.

The sunshine coming in through the windows lit the room. Lara was sprawled out on the bed like a cat. Walking over to the side of the bed, Bram looked down at her. Wisps of hair spread across the pillow like a spider's web, and her face was buried in the covers. The sheets were tucked around her, hugging her form. He could see the curve of her waist to her hip, and down to her small feet. It made him desperately want to snuggle up behind her and hold her in his arms.

Bram felt very protective of her, and could not control the feelings and emotions stirring within him. He felt as if he had known her a lifetime, yet he barely knew her at all. Days had felt like years when they were confined in the dungeon. He could not distinguish whether his feelings for her were friendly or something more. All he knew was that he would protect her with his life, and cut down any man who treated her poorly.

Lara stirred, feeling someone watching her. She slowly opened her eyes and looked about the room. Bram had been staring down at her; his eyebrows were furrowed and he looked forlorn. His close proximity to her made her breath quicken and she wanted to jump out of the bed and put distance between them. Bram gave her a soft smile before he spoke.

"It is time to wake. I have brought ye something to eat," he said handing her an apple.

As he reached to hand her the apple, Lara noticed how calloused his hands were and all of the tiny little scars along the backs of them. His hands were twice as big as hers, and, she imagined, quite strong as well. They were the hands of a warrior.

Lara grabbed the apple and took a small bite, its juice beading on her lips.

Bram's heart fluttered at the site of Lara licking the juice from her lips. How sweet they would taste if only he was given the opportunity. At that moment he wanted nothing more than to scoop her into his arms and kiss her.

Bram scolded himself. He needed to get his wits about him. She was married, and even if her husband was a bloody bastard, he would not dishonor Lara by causing her to break her vows. He made a pledge to himself that he would push these feelings aside and keep his promise to her to escort her home; and for his sake, the sooner the better.

As they left the town, the terrain changed dramatically. The ground became uneven and rocky, causing the horse to slow its pace as they rode up the steep hillside. Lara heard the sound of gravel and rocks as they tumbled down the cliff behind them. Once they reached the top of the hill, Lara looked out over the land. It was magnificent.

Spreading before her were rolling hills and high mountains, lush greenery and a dark dense forest as far as she could see, known by many as the Black Forest. It was rumored that not only was the forest home to a gang of highwaymen, but that it was haunted as well. Not many dared to enter the woods from the south. Most Lowlanders traveled around the forest to reach the northern territory. In the center of the Black Forest was

Loch Lomond. Once they reached the loch they would be safely in Highland territory.

A chill shook Lara to her core as they approached the mouth of the forest. It was as dark as the night sky, with not a speck of light shining through the heavily leaved branches overhead.

"Will we need to camp in there tonight?" she asked, feeling chill bumps creep up her arm as they approached the darkness.

"Aye. But I ken what path to take to stay away from unwanted visitors that may be lurking in these woods. Dinna worry, lass," he said as he held her tighter in his arms.

Holding her so close to his body made it much more difficult to keep his hands from wandering. Bram stirred in the saddle as he immensely enjoyed the feeling of her backside against his front.

"But the howls in the distance - are ye no' afraid?"

"They be only wolves, lass. Nothing more."

"Do ye no' believe in the legends of these woods?"

Bram chuckled.

"Lass, who do ye think the legends were meant to scare? 'Twas the Highlanders who told those stories, to keep enemies wary of entering these woods."

His confidence gave Lara a little sense of relief but not enough to calm her completely. She kept her eyes trained firmly on their surroundings.

"Honestly, lass, there is nay a thing to worry about. We will rest once we reach Loch Lomond."

Cresting the last wooded hill, the sight of Loch Lomond at the bottom of the valley was far more beautiful than Lara had imagined. The sunlight twinkled off the surface of the water like tiny stars fallen to earth. As they reached the loch, they dismounted and rested for a short while, as Bram had promised.

The hot sun beat down on them. Lara did not recall a hotter summer than this, and there was no evidence that rain had fallen in weeks. The grass beneath them was dry and beginning to brown. Within the hour, they once again continued their journey to Stearns Castle.

Chapter 11

Stearns Castle was built on the highest point of a hill that overlooked the village. Its outer stone walls stood tall and intimidating, easily twenty or thirty feet high, and looked as if they could touch the clouds. Lacking windows, the castle looked forbidding.

As they approached the gate, a guard stopped them from entering. When the guard turned and looked at Lara he almost lost his footing. His jaw slightly fell open and his gaze looked dazed, as if someone had hit him over the head. Without hesitation, the guard opened the gates and allowed them entry.

"Mistress? What are ye doing here, my lady?" the guard asked.

"Adrian, I must insist on speaking with my father. Where is he? My husband has done something terrible."

"I am afraid, my lady, that yer father is no' here. He has traveled with John to Bergen."

"Bergen, Norway?" Lara raised her voice puzzled why her father would have traveled so far.

"Aye, my lady."

Lara struggled to offer him a friendly smile. Without her father, she knew not what to do. If Dermot learned she had returned home, he would surely come for her. Suddenly, she felt a bout of nausea come over her.

Bram quietly walked up behind her and placed his hand on her shoulder. She turned a solemn face to him. She did not want to cry. Not now. Not ever. She was glad that he did not show her pity. Instead, his slight smile lifted her spirits. His eyes were the color of honey, a light amber shade. She mused that she hadn't noticed them before. They reminded her of a warm autumn day, just as the leaves began to turn gold.

"Thank ye fer bringing me home, Bram."

"Lara, I promised ye my protection and Highlanders dinna break our promises," Bram curled his lip and gave her a genuine smile.

"I suppose ye will be leaving now?" she asked. Sadness crept inside her heart at having to say goodbye. There was so much more she wanted to learn about him. They had shared an experience few others survived. Their acquaintance was short, but their bond was strong.

"Aye."

"I shall never forget ye and yer kindness," Lara said as she stepped up on the tips of her toes and softly planted a kiss to his rough cheek. "God speed," she whispered in his ear before lowering her feet back to the ground.

Bram turned to mount his horse. Lara wanted to ask him to stay, to at least rest for a night, but she did not.

Just as he mounted the horse, a woman called out to them from a distance. Hiking up her dress, she ran towards them at a full sprint. As the woman came closer, her features became more distinct. She was an older woman, dressed in a plain brown dress covered by a white linen apron tied around her plump waist. Her grey hair was tightly braided except for a few loose tendrils that flew in the wind. As she drew closer, Lara recognized the old woman. It was Moira, her clan's head cook.

Breathlessly, Moira cried out, "My lady, my lady!"

Lara veered to face her and greet the old woman.

"Moira, what is it?" Lara asked.

With no response, Moira swung her arms around Lara. Lara squeezed her equally as tight. Stepping out of her embrace, Lara looked into the old woman's eyes. She had aged since Lara had last seen her. Deep wrinkles creased across her forehead and her eye lids sagged as if she had not slept in a month.

"Oh be gone wit ye, ye auld brute," Moira snapped at the guard, as if he was intruding on a private conversation. "Oh, my lady. Tis good to see ye. Ach, dinna they feed her at that castle? Ye are skin and bones!"

"Tis a long and dreadful story, Moira. But I must ask. Do ye ken when my father is expected to return?"

"I dinna ken." Lara's look of despair caused Moira to frown. "I'm sorry lass, but in order to see him, I'm afraid ye would have to travel to Norway; a ridiculous notion. Nay, ye will stay right here and wait fer him to return. I'll no' have ye traveling that far by yerself to find him." Moira said with a comforting pat.

"But Moira, I must go. I must speak to him. Why has he traveled so far?"

Moira eyed Bram suspiciously.

"Ye can trust him, Moira," Lara reassured her.

"My lady, strange things have happened since ye left. If yer father kenned I ken anything of his plans he would have strung me up from the gallows."

"Whatever ye ken Moira, I promise yer secret is safe wit' me," Lara promised.

Moira looked around, making sure no one could hear what she was about to reveal.

"I was cleaning up the stairs as I usually do. Yer father and John were in the library talking. I overhead 'em. I dinna go eavesdropping deliberately, ye ken. They said that the King of Norway was dying; said that because he has nay any heirs that there is nay one to take the throne but his brother whom he had been feuding. Yer father plans to propose John as his vassal to take the throne."

"Vassal?"

"Aye. They plan to claim John as his cousin. Oh, my lady, if the people of Norway ken they were tricked, the country would be in turmoil. The war between Norway and Denmark could then cause war with England and France and that be nay good fer any of us."

Bram thought about Lara's predicament and what this would mean for Scotland.

"I will take ye," he offered

"What?" Lara turned and asked as if she had not heard him.

"I will take ye to Norway to see yer father. I have some distant relatives there on my Mam's side."

"Bram, we can nay go to Norway. Moira is right. 'Tis an insane idea. Bergen is a royal castle. We cannae just walk into the gates and demand an audience."

Bram smiled at her, "Aye lass, we can."

Lara felt perplexed. She paced back and forth, her brow rising and falling. Bram and Moira both patiently waited until Lara stopped and looked from one to the other.

"King! John to be king! He has nay royal blood and he is no' even Norwegian."

"I dinna ken what I can say, my lady," Moira replied.

"Then there is only one thing I can do. We will go to Norway and seek my father. Perhaps all will be revealed once I arrive."

"God be wit ye both," Moira said, holding onto Lara's hand.

Bram knew that their route would take them further east, to the city of Aberdeen, the nearest port. From there, they would travel by boat across the sea and arrive in Norway a few days later.

"Lass, we have a long journey ahead of us. We should leave now, if ye truly wish to go," Bram suggested.

Lara turned and hugged Moira one last time. Bram knew there were no easy roads to take north to Aberdeen, nor were they safe. They would be traveling through rough terrain and alongside steep hills, but his worst fear was crossing paths with the English.

Chapter 12

Dark clouds covered the sky. Though it was mid-day, the sky turned dark as night as a raging storm caused a heavy downpour. Bram offered Lara his plaid and tightly wrapped her in it. Even with the plaid, she was soaked to the bone.

As thunder and lightning struck, Lara buried her head deeper into Bram's hold. As the air cooled, her teeth started to chatter. She felt Bram wrap his arm around her tighter, but instead of snuggling into him as she so desperately wanted, she sat upright, keeping a small space between them.

Lara wanted to ask Bram to stop in order for her to stretch out her legs and perhaps warm herself by a fire, but she remained silent. The chances of finding dry wood were slim. Everything was wet. The ground was soft and muddy, causing the horse to slow.

In the forefront of her mind was speculation about how her father would react when he learned everything that had befallen her. She wondered if he would take vengeance upon her husband, or send her back. Her whole life Lara had wondered why her father was so harsh towards her but so lenient with John. Perhaps he was upset that she was a girl, and not one of the many sons that he had wanted.

Her mother, Elsa, only gave birth to the two of them, and after that refused to lay with him again. He bedded other women and blamed Elsa for his acts of adultery. William was a hard man, even towards Elsa. It was only after her death that he expressed his love for her and built the wall around his heart. It was John he turned his attentions to, forcing him to study and train until he was stumbling with sleep deprivation.

Lara imagined that a great king would do no less, but the thought of her brother becoming a king was still something that she could not fathom. To her, he was still nothing more than her older brother; he was selfish, and oftentimes made fun of her. But a king? Someone who would rule over and go into great battles? The idea of her brother doing such things was unthinkable.

Lara and Bram rode north along the coast. As the rain continued to fall, Bram steered the horse into the trees along the mountainside, hoping it would lessen the rain falling on them. The wind changed, blowing rain that felt like needles were piercing his face. He prayed that the storm would stop soon and that they could find shelter before nightfall. They would certainly become ill, sleeping outside in wet clothing with no fire to warm them. He worried about Lara as she uncontrollably shook in his arms, her teeth vigorously chattering. Desperately, he searched for a dry place to take cover from the cold rain.

As they continued through the forest of young oaks and pines, Bram spotted a small opening along the rock face. He let out a long sigh of relief and thanked God for answering his prayers. The entrance to the cavern was so small that he almost missed it. It did not look deep, but would offer sufficient protection.

"Lass," Bram whispered in a gentle tone. She had fallen asleep against his chest. He did not want to wake her. He immensely enjoyed holding her in his arms, but he did not want her cause of death to be exposure to the elements. He spoke softly into her ear,

"Lara, I have found us cover from the rain."

Lara raised her head and opened her eyes. Bram dismounted and walked the horse under a group of tall pines, stringing the reins around a sturdy branch before helping Lara down. He extended his hand to her, but she did not accept it.

Hurt filled the caverns of his heart when she sidestepped him, evading his gesture.

When Bram reached out for her, Lara was inclined to put her small hand into his. But there was no reason for it. She had no trouble walking on her own and accepting the gesture was inappropriate under the circumstances, especially if she wanted to maintain her distance. Over the past several days, she had noticed these small gestures Bram offered, and they only confused her. He was not behaving as she had expected. He was supposed to be a brave Highland warrior but instead, he was acting like a besotted fool.

Bram's mood quickly turned grim.

"There's a cavern just o'er there. Go on inside. I will meet ye there in a bit."

Bram stalked off in search of dry wood, leaving the lass to attend to her needs. After several long moments of searching, he found a few dry logs under a pile of thick brush. Gathering them under one arm, he walked back over to the horse to grab the saddlebags. Once he had everything he needed, he walked back to the cave.

Lara unraveled the wet plaid around her as it no longer offered her warmth and sat on the cold ground. She rubbed her hands up and down her arms. It wasn't very long before Bram returned with an arm full of logs.

Dropping the logs with a hard thud, Bram sat down and dug through his bag. His brows furrowed and the forlorn look on his face told Lara that her dismissal must have angered him, but she had not the faintest idea why.

As he emptied the bag onto the ground she saw the reason for his expression. All of the peat and food, other than a single apple, had been spoiled by the rain.

"Damnation," he growled and threw the logs of soaked peat through the mouth of the cave into the rain.

With nothing more than an apple left, Bram knew there would not be enough to fill their bellies. But food, for now, would have to wait. His first concern was starting the fire to warm Lara. Taking out a flint, he tried to light the half soaked wood. It took several attempts until a fire sparked to life. Bram stood and removed his tunic and placed it on a rock near the fire to dry. He sat down in front of it across from Lara and allowed the fire to warm him.

"Ye need to get out of yer wet clothes."

"Pardon me!"

"Ye will get sick if ye stay in them and ye will get nay benefit from sitting next to the fire all wet."

"I will do nay such thing. No' in front of ye!" she retorted.

"I am no' trying to take advantage of the situation. If ye will only see the right of it, I only have yer best interest at heart. I am no' a spiteful mon, Lara. But I will no' sit here and allow ye to be irrational over the matter. If ye prefer, once the plaid dries ye can take off yer gown and cover yerself wit' the plaid until yer dress is dry enough to put back on."

Lara did not at all like being treated as a child, nor did she like the idea of sitting with nothing but a plaid to cover her, but she knew he spoke the truth. She was shivering in her wet gown, and did not know how much longer she could withstand the cold. The flames of the fire offered some warmth, but it was not enough. She felt the chill in her bones.

Bram took the apple and sliced it in half with his dirk. He handed her one of the halves, and in two bites he finished the other.

"I will need to go out and get us some food before we lose the light. It will soon be too dark" Bram informed her as he stood up.

"But it is still raining out," Lara said.

Bram smiled at her show of concern. But he had spent many days in rain such as this, and he had little choice in the matter but to find food.

"I will be fine, lass. Stay here and keep yerself warm. I will nay be long."

Lara crept closer to the fire and clutched the plaid. It appeared dry enough to wrap around her. Waiting until she could no longer hear Bram's footsteps outside the cave, she slid her gown off her shoulders. Its silk fabric clung to her body. Slipping out of the gown, she stood naked in front of the fire for a moment. Once she was warm, she donned the plaid, doing the best she could to cover every inch of her exposed skin.

After a long while, Bram had still not returned and Lara's stomach ached. She decided there was only one thing to do: find her own meal. But how?

Digging though Bram's bag, she found a small dagger in the side pocket. Taking the dagger, Lara tightened the top of the plaid around her bosom so that it would not fall down. Creeping towards the exit, Lara poked her head out and called out for Bram. No answer. The rain had stopped, so Lara decided to go in search of something, anything she could eat. Quieting her movements, she heard a rustling noise coming from a small bush. Taking one step closer to it, she listened to the noise and waited. Holding the dagger up like her brother had shown her, she waited until the creature showed itself.

The bush shook and a small hare jumped out into the open. Lara flung the dagger towards it hitting her mark. Bending down, Lara picked up the dead rabbit and carried it back inside the cave.

Shortly after, Bram returned with a small skinned boar hanging upside down from a branch. Rainwater dripped off him and puddled under his feet.

"Ye must be freezing. Best ye come sit by the fire to warm yerself before ye succumb to fever," Lara cautioned.

Bram laughed wickedly; its sound echoing through the small cavern.

"I can only think of one way to warm a mon in these circumstances," he said, giving her a meaningful smile.

"Please dinna look at me that way," Lara replied turning her head away from him and tightening the plaid around her shoulders.

"Look at ye like what?"

"Like I am a harlot and no' a married woman."

Bram slapped his leg and chuckled.

"Ach lass. Ye think I mean to bed ye. I promise that as tempting as that may sound, I only be talking about drowning myself in a tankard of whisky," he replied shaking his head at the lass's silly assertion.

Lara felt like a fool, embarrassing herself with her assumption. She shifted in place as she became increasingly uncomfortable with his laughter as he looked at her. It was bad enough that she was sitting half naked in *his* plaid as she waited for her dress to dry.

She did not think that believing he wished to bed her was such a ridiculous notion. After all, he had given plenty of indications that he wanted more than just a friendship. She considered the thought that perhaps she was wrong. Perhaps he did not care for her in that manner. In truth, she should be pleased, for if he did have feelings for her, there was nothing either of them could do about it.

As Bram sat down, he noticed the dead hare lying on a slab of stone.

In surprise, he asked, "Where the bloody hell did that come from?"

"I caught it. Ye were gone so long I thought perhaps ye could no' find food."

"Ye? Ye caught that? How?" he asked still surprised that the lass could perform such a task - and without a weapon!

"I found yer dagger and hit him like a bow would hit a moving target."

"Where the bloody hell did ye learn that?"

"My brother. He taught me many useful things. I may be a lass but I am verra capable of taking care of myself," she stated very proudly as she handed the dead creature to Bram.

Lara watched Bram as he cleaned, then began roasting, the rabbit and small boar. It did not take long until they were fully cooked. With the small dagger he kept tucked in his boot, he carved the meat from the bone and handed her a slice.

"How did ye catch that wit' out a bow?" Lara asked, never seeing a man catch a boar with only his hands. Boars were very strong and quick and could jump right out of a predator's grasp.

"I am good at hunting. When I was a lad, my father and uncle would take my brother Rory, my cousin Ewan, and me hunting wit' out weapons. They taught us how to use the land and use what is around us to hunt and survive. In hunting, as in fighting, ye need strategy and can no' always depend on yer weapon, fer the only weapon ye truly have is yer wit."

"Ye dinna talk much about yer brother. Are ye close to him?"

"My brother and I are two verra different people. What about ye? Are ye close to yer brother?"

"We were close when we were young, but as he got older he grew distant."

"If he is no' blood to the throne, why do ye suppose he could be passed off as the King's only successor?"

"I dinna ken. When my father lived in Norway he met my mum and married her, returning to her home in Scotland. He never talked about Norway or anything of his or her past. After the death of young Lady Margaret the Queen of the Scots, he began traveling back and forth stating that his interest in Norway was purely business. Perhaps he decided to offer John as a loyal subject, worthy of the crown."

"Dinna ye think it odd, that ye only found out after yer father married ye off to Laird Moray?"

Lara thought hard on his question. Searching her memories, she did not recall any announcement or talks of John ever taking over the throne. What were the reasons behind waiting for her to be married off to announce such a thing? And why would they not have invited her? So many unanswered questions danced around in her head. She wondered what other secrets they had kept from her. She was almost afraid to find out.

Chapter 13

Over the next several days, Lara regaled Bram with stories about her past, and he found himself sharing bits and pieces of his as well, though leaving out certain details of his cavalier love life. The more time Bram spent with her, the more he came to want her. He had honestly never spent this much time with a woman and he certainly never had been inclined to talk to one outside of everyday conversation. But with Lara, he found himself truly listening to her. And he was enthralled by every word.

Bram was fascinated by how well educated she was. Not scholarly by any means, as she knew nothing about reading or writing, but by the world around her. She paid a great deal of attention to the art of healing, the teachings of the church, and even some matters of politics. She was a free spirit, and regardless of what had happened to her, she loved life. He was completely baffled by her.

Bram did not know how a woman could have so much resolve and determination with her history. In her situation, he would have expected the lass to be docile and submissive; she was anything but. She had a wicked tongue and was a little too opinionated for a lass. He could see why Dermot thought her to be defiant, and the thought put a mischievous smile on his face.

What he admired the most about her was her heart. The way she spoke of fond memories and of her dreams made Bram think about his own life and unfulfilled dreams. Bram found himself suddenly regretting his promise. It was not his promise to protect her; it was knowing how this journey would end.

Bram and Lara crossed the stone bridge in Aberdeen which led into the market square. People crowded the market, buying and trading their goods, while a group of minstrels played their instruments.

Suddenly Lara called out, "Watch out!"

Instantly, Bram pulled tightly on the reins causing the horse to halt. Bram felt Lara hug him tighter around the waist as she had almost been tossed off the large beast. Unexpectedly, a wee lad ran out in front of them being chased by three other lads.

"Bloody hell!" he cursed under his breath. "Ye coulda been killed ye hellions!" Bram shouted, but the lads could not hear him over the crowd's noise.

Bram righted himself in the saddle, and directed the horse down the road.

"Have ye been here before?" Lara asked.

"Aye. 'Tis similar to Dumfries, only the goods imported here are verra different. They come by sea from other countries such as the Orient and the Holy Land."

"What sorts of things?"

Bram looked down at Lara. Her eyes were wide, looking at the carts as they passed by them. Bram smiled at her and her child-like expressions. She looked as if she were devouring a sweet roll with her eyes.

"Weapons, fine silks, exotic foods, and precious stones."

"Do ye suppose the journey to Norway will take long?"

"Aye. Tis two or three days' travel across the sea. We will follow the river to the harbor, then board a vessel that will take us there."

Once they reached port, Lara could not contain her anticipation. She felt nervous and excited all at once. The only ships she had seen before were rowboats along the lochs. She marveled at the size of these ships.

Leaving their horse behind, Lara followed Bram up the long gangplank to the main deck of the vessel. Several other passengers followed closely behind.

Aboard was a small crew of no more than ten plus the captain. Once everyone was on board, Bram and Lara moved to the stern of the boat. Three members of the ship's crew pulled hard on a rope, turning the yardarm high on the mast. Within moments, the sail dropped and the wind caught hold, causing the sail to flutter. The captain called out the order to bring up the anchor. When the anchor was lifted, Lara felt the waves crashing into the side of the boat as they turned, bearing north and east towards Norway.

"Lara, ye may want to hold on or sit down. The ride can be verra bumpy and it is easy to get sick from the rocking if ye are nay used to it," Bram suggested.

"Nay, I will be fine. Thank ye."

Peering over the side of the hull, Lara gazed into the deep blue waters. It was so different from the Firth of Clyde near Castle Foley. Darkness clouded the sea floor. The only thing she could see was her own reflection staring back at her. The water rippled as the bow cut through the surface like a sharp knife. The open ocean was like nothing she had ever seen. It looked endless. She could not tell where the ocean ended and the sky began.

As the wind blew stronger, the ship gained speed, and Lara's hair waved wildly in the wind. She closed her eyes and felt the breeze and cool mist on her face. She thought that this must have been what a bird felt like when taking flight.

Over the next hour, Lara watched and listened to the crewmen as they told tales of pirates and selkies. Their animated expressions and dramatic gestures made the stories come to life as they acted out each scene. Once they finished with their tales, Lara turned to ask Bram whether he believed if their fables were true, but he was no longer sitting by her side. Lara looked over her shoulder in search of Bram and found him standing against the hull looking out across the sea.

Lara realized she had grown quite fond of him. She found herself smiling every time he was near. It was hard not to. He had offered her his protection, his comfort, and his friendship, and there was no denying the feelings that were developing inside her. She tried to will them away and think of him only as her escort, or like a brother; anything other than the wanton thoughts and feelings she was having about him.

Like a young lass, she found herself daydreaming of what could have been. Distracted by her wandering thoughts, she had a hard time keeping her mind in the here and now. Her heart hammered in her chest as she secretly watched him. Even though he was a beast in height and strength, he was chivalrous and steadfast, and possibly the most handsome man she had ever laid her eyes upon.

Lara found herself yearning for his kisses, for him to wrap his protective arms around her and shield her from the world. But her mind overruled her heart. While she wanted to allow herself the freedom to open her heart to him, common sense brought her back to reality; that even though her marriage had not been consummated, bound by law and contract, she still belonged to Dermot. Only Father Bolbec, who'd performed the ceremony, had the authority to annul the marriage. Even if she could prove that there was no coupling between them, many years' acquaintance with Father Bolbec told her that he would not be easily swayed. His position gave him the authority to arbitrarily set rules and laws outside of what the

Pope would declare, and pass judgment on what he believed was unholy or against the laws of the church. Lara knew his decisions often had little to do with the church, and were more about power and control.

Lara stood and began walking towards Bram. As she took a small step, she began to feel her head spin and her stomach turn. Stopping for a moment, she drew in a long breath and started to walk again. Feeling a bit wobbly, she slowed her pace. As she stood beside Bram, she instantly put her hand to her stomach.

"What ails ye?" Bram asked with concern etched on his face.

The world started to spin and Lara's stomach felt as if it was tossing back and forth along with the ship. She opened her mouth to explain but strained to speak as she felt bile rising in the back of her throat.

"Ye dinna look too well, Lass. Yer skin is pale," Bram said as he raised his hand to her forehead. "And ye feel as cold as the winter air."

"Must...stop...rocking," Lara mumbled as her hand went to her mouth. "Please, stop the ship from rocking," she pleaded.

Bram chuckled.

"Lass, I can no' stop the ship from rocking back and forth. We are in the middle of the sea. I warned ye that ye were goin' to get sick," he reminded her.

Lara could see the smug, satisfied grin on his face. Now was not the time to be arrogant and thick-headed, she thought, as she saw him trying to cover his smile.

"Ye are finding enjoyment in this, nay?"

"Aye. Dinna say I dinna warn ye lass. Most people think they won't be affected by the motion of the sea, but most of the time the sea wins," he replied.

Lara's stomach clenched. Holding on tightly to the railing, she retched over the side of the ship. As she continued to empty her stomach, Lara could feel one of Bram's hands on her back and the other holding her hair up and out of the way. After a quarter of an hour, Lara felt her stomach ease and slumped down to sit on the deck. Bram joined her, scooting himself beside her. He handed her a handkerchief so she could wipe her mouth.

Against her better judgment, Lara leaned into him. Bram instinctively wrapped his arm around her. As much as she wanted to, Lara did not allow herself to take comfort in his arms. Within three days or so, he would be gone from her life, and she could not bear the disappointment she was already beginning to feel at the thought of leaving him. If only things were different, and she could express her feelings; but she knew she couldn't. Instead, she would lock them away in the deepest recesses of her heart.

Bram's humor faded as Lara rested against his chest and in his arms. They were still two days away from port and there were no healers on board to ease her discomfort. He had only hoped that rest would offer her the comfort she needed.

Bram did not understand why Lara couldn't see how he felt about her. He had tried to be agreeable and careful of her, but apparently it wasn't enough. He was becoming angry with himself. He was a coward.

There were so many things he wanted to tell her, but he was either too proud or too daft to say the words. He had never felt this way about a woman, and he didn't like having so little control over his own heart. She was opinionated, stubborn, brash, irrational, and completely illogical, but he loved her with every fiber of his being. He was certain of it. But did she love him in return? Aye, she was married, but their union was just a minor inconvenience, and one that he would make certain was rectified.

As she lay there in his arms, Bram could still smell the lavender scented soap she'd used in her hair days ago. Her nearness was the sweetest torture he had ever endured. He would do anything to be with her, even ride across Europe to Italy and demand that the Pope terminate her marriage contract; or take his blade to that bastard husband of hers, leaving her a widow. He would ride to the ends of the earth and back for her. But first, he needed to win her heart.

In the following two days at sea, Lara's condition worsened. She threw up several times and was not able to keep much food down. Bram encouraged her to rest as much as she could, as it was the only relief she had. Lara swore that she would never set foot on a boat again.

As if angels were answering her prayers, she heard the captain call out to his men, "Ease off the line laddies, 'tis land ahead."

Lara looked over the side of the hull. The inland waters were as blue as the brightest bluebells she had ever seen. The water reflected the land above the shore like a perfect mirror. The pine-covered, hilly land looked much different than the rocky terrain she was accustomed to. But it was the thought of standing on solid land that brought her the most joy.

143

Heading into the channel, the crew lowered the sail and dropped anchor. After they'd docked and the passengers had disembarked, the captain and his entourage went barreling down the boarding plank, carrying with them barrels and boxes of fresh supplies.

"How long do ye think it will take us to get to Bergen?" Lara asked Bram, hoping to reach her father soon.

"By tomorrow evening, if all goes well," Bram replied.

Lara was elated by his answer. Finally, after several weeks, she could seek justice for Dermot's treachery.

Chapter 14

"Where is he?" Dermot hollered at the guard.

Dermot and five of his guards had ridden four days from Foley Castle to Stearns to demand an audience with Laird Fergusson for the rights to Lara's dowry. Upon their departure after the wedding ceremony, he had only been given a trunk full of worthless trinkets. Laird Fergusson had told him about the treasure, and promised that Dermot would possess it in due time. But Dermot was determined not to wait any longer.

Now, with Lara's unexpected disappearance from the English prison, he found it necessary to retrieve the remainder of her belongings before the truth got out. Of course, if the Fergussons knew the truth of it, they would surely deny him his percentage of the treasure and kill him on the spot.

"I am afraid, my Laird, that Laird Fergusson is nay here. He has gone to Norway," the guard stuttered and shrunk in fear.

At that moment, so consumed by rage, Dermot wanted nothing more than to pull out his dirk and put it through the man's throat. He struggled for restraint.

Dermot knew that he needed to get to Norway and get his hands on that treasure before they found out the truth about Lara. He started to regret his hasty decision to send her off with the English guards. Dermot had not thought what to do if Alban, Lara's father, demanded to see her.

"I am sure, my Laird, that if ye make haste, ye can catch up wit' yer wife."

Dermot's eyes narrowed. Grabbing the guard's collar with both hands, he forcefully pushed him against the wall and lifted him into the air.

"What do ye mean catch up wit' my wife?" he demanded.

"To…to Norway, my Laird. She left here two days ago," the guard said as he began to shake.

"Lara! Lara was here? Impossible!" Dermot roared.

"I speak the truth, my Laird. Saw her wit' my own eyes."

Dermot thought on the man's words. How could she have escaped? Was someone helping her? Did her father already know what he'd done?

"Was she traveling by herself?" he growled.

"Nay, my Laird. She had a mon accompanying her."

"What did she say?" Dermot asked.

"Nothing, my Laird. I did no' speak to her. Moira the housemaid did."

Worry came over Dermot that she'd already revealed what he had done. He did not trust the guard and believed he was lying to protect her. He tightened his hold on the man for a moment longer before suddenly letting go. The guard fell to the ground, holding his arm up over his head, waiting for a blow, but Dermot just stared at the man.

He needed to leave, and fast. If Lara was two days ahead of him, he had little time. He would either have to catch up with her in Aberdeen or reach Norway before she arrived. If she did arrive before him, all would be lost.

Dermot ordered his guards back to the horses. Jumping into the saddle, he kicked his horse's sides hard, forcing it to take off at a full gallop.

Looking out the window slit, Moira watched as Laird Moray and his men threatened the guard, Adrian, in front of the gate. Pacing back and forth inside the kitchen, she prayed that Adrian did not reveal too much information. If he did, he would surely lead Dermot right to Lara. If that happened, Moira knew, something terrible would happen to her. She cursed herself for not saying anything to Adrian about keeping Lara's arrival secret, but she'd had no cause to believe that Dermot would be following.

"Damn that mon," she said to herself, as she watched Laird Moray and his men mount their horses and take off in a northerly direction. She feared the worst. She quickly left the kitchen and scurried out the door towards the battlement.

"Adrian," Moira called out to him. "Was that Laird Moray?" she asked, wanting to verify what she had seen.

"Aye. He came to see Laird Fergusson."

"Ye dinna tell him about Lara, did ye?" Moira asked with pleading eyes.

"Aye. Tis his wife. Why shouldnae he ken?"

"Oh Adrian, what have ye done, ye daft fool?" Moira bellowed, and looked out the gates.

Her heart squeezed with angst. She worried deeply for her mistress. Moira sent up silent prayers, that God would watch over Lara and offer His guidance and protection.

Chapter 15

In Lara's weakened condition, Bram held onto her arm as they walked down the gangplank and onto the sandy shore. Her legs wobbled as she walked. Slightly hunched over, she held her stomach with her arms. Bram found a slab of rock upon which she could sit while he ran over to the shops across the dirt road from the docks to inquire about food and an inn where Lara could rest.

The port city was still several miles south of the castle, and Bram knew they would never make it before nightfall; certainly not with Lara in her current condition.

"Here, drink this. It will make ye feel better," he said as he handed her a tankard of ale. "I secured a room fer us tonight so ye can rest. We can leave for Bergen first thing when ye feel better."

"Nay. I am fine. I wish to go now," she protested.

"Lass, ye will do as I say. Ye are no' well, ye stubborn lass, and I refuse to travel wit' ye any further while ye are sick. Ye will eat and sleep, and until ye do so, we will no' be leaving."

"Bram, I did no' come this far to wait another day. I am going wit or wit out ye."

"And how will ye get there? Walk?"

"Aye. If I must."

"Ye are the most infuriating, irrational woman in all of Scotland!"

"Well, then it is a good thing we are no' in Scotland," she retorted.

"Lass, I will no' say it again. Ye are no' going anywhere until ye get better, even if I have to tie ye to the bed," Bram said clenching his teeth.

"Ye thick-headed barbarian! Ye can no' chain me like chattel and order me around."

"Dinna tempt me, lass."

Lara struck him a fierce look. In a fit of anger, Lara stood, but quickly plopped back down onto the bench trying to regain her bearings.

"See, ye are too weak to even stand. Now stay here. I will get us the room. A fine meal and a hot bath will make ye feel better," he said as he walked away.

The thought of a nice hot bath did sound appealing in her current state. As much as she hated to admit it, she knew Bram was right; but she had been traveling for almost a week, and she needed rest. If Dermot and his men had set sail towards Norway, they would most certainly catch up to them before arriving in Bergen. That fact frightened her more than anything.

She realized then that her anger towards Bram helped shield her fear. She wanted to show bravery, but it was a ruse. Not only was Lara frightened of what would transpire at Bergen, but also of her feelings towards Bram. With each passing day, they grew stronger and harder to resist.

After obtaining a room for the night, Bram walked to the stables within the small town to see if he could acquire a horse. Inside the stable was a small lad who was tending to the horses. At that moment, Bram was grateful to his mother for the hours she made him spend studying the Old Norse language, as the lad spoke little Gaelic.

After bargaining with the lad, he managed to acquire a fine stallion. Handing the lad a few coins, Bram instructed him to have the horse fed and ready for travel by morning. Once he'd completed his business, he returned to Lara's side on the rock.

Even sick, she was beautiful. Her hair flowed down her back and looked as soft as silk. And the curves under her dress made his skin crawl wanting to touch her. Bram could not ignore the pounding in his chest as he drew closer to her. His palms began to sweat, and he could feel a dull ache in his groin.

"The lad at the stables mentioned the castle was no' too far from here; only a days' ride."

"Have ye found us a room?"

"Aye. We can go there now if ye like," he said as he held his arm out for her.

As Lara stood, Bram paused and turned to her. As much as she drove him mad, he knew that he could never stay angry with her. Holding her in his arms, his desire for her burned within his veins, and for once he saw her look to him with the same yearning.

"Ye are so beautiful," he said as he leaned down to kiss her, but at the very last moment, Lara turned her head to the side.

Lara felt stunned by his comment, even though his words made her heart beat fast and hard in her chest. She did not know how to respond. She never believed herself to be beautiful, and no man had ever told her that before. Dermot had told her that she was plain, and Lara easily believed him. But now, looking into Bram's eyes, she could tell that he'd believed what he'd said.

More than anything, she wanted to tell him that over the past week she had fallen deeply and passionately in love with him, but she could not bring herself to say the words. It would only make the pain greater, knowing they could never be together. And to make matters worse, he had tried to kiss her. As much as she wanted his lips on hers, she had to deny her feelings, and him. What she said next, she knew, she would certainly regret for the rest of her life.

"Please dinna say things like that to me. If ye think I have any sort of romantic feelings fer ye, ye are surely mistaken."

"I dinna mean to offend ye, lass. I only speak the truth."

"Ye should nay talk that way to a married woman. Ye and I can ne'er be together, cannae ye see that?"

Bram had thought that over the past week he had softened her heart towards him, but in truth, her actions and words indicated that she wanted nothing to do with him. He felt like a fool for thinking otherwise. Nodding his head to acknowledge her rejection, he suggested heading to the inn.

Once inside the room, Lara and Bram moved about, each doing what they could to ignore the other. Lara felt that if she did not say something soon she would implode. She felt more uncomfortable with his ignoring her than his attempt to kiss her.

"Will food and hot water be brought up to the room?" she asked, wanting the break the silence between them.

"Aye. It should be here soon. Ye can take the first bath."

"And where will ye be?"

"I will wait down in the tavern. I could use a drink or two," he said, thinking that it would take more than a tankard or two to rid himself of his utter humiliation.

At a knock on the door, Bram crossed the room and allowed two maids to enter. Each one of them carried a steaming bucket of hot water in each hand. A third maid followed close behind with a tray of meat and bread. Bram snatched up a few pieces of meat and a slice of the bread and headed down to the tavern to give Lara her privacy.

Lara waited until the maids had gone before removing her dress and stepping into the bath. Once inside, she leaned her head back and closed

154

her eyes. If heaven existed, at this very moment, this was it.

Bram sat at a table in the corner of the tavern staring into his mug. He thought about what tomorrow would bring. After he delivered Lara to her father, he would head back to Dunakin. He was anxious to see his family and his boys. While thinking about Lara, he could not shake the feeling that something was wrong with this whole situation. He was curious why her father was so eager for his son to become king, knowing that his son had no royal blood. Should the people of Norway learn their king was a fraud, they could abandon their loyalty for Norway and might seek a new alliance with Denmark, which would cause the English to intervene and take control of the country. Any further English power, and King Edward would double his army and be able to kill every Scot in the Highlands. What bothered him the most about this situation was why so many secrets were kept from Lara.

It came to him suddenly, like being hit in the head with a rock. The English threat must have been the reason for keeping Lara in the dark. Her father must not have wanted her caught in the middle of a battle if it came to that, but Dermot's role made no sense. What was Lara's dowry, and was it really worth killing for?

Too many unanswered questions clouded Bram's mind. He feared that whatever Lara's father was keeping from her put her in grave danger. He figured that Dermot must have found out his secret, and that was the reason he tried to rid himself of her. That would explain why he had sent men out after her. With no plan or army to help protect them, Bram and Lara were on their own and they could very well be heading right into the mouth of a dragon.

Chapter 16

Lara took a deep breath as she and Bram stood just outside the gates that led into the bailey of the Norse Castle. People rushed to and from the open courtyard as the gate guards stood watch. As they stepped under the portcullis and past the gate house, they entered into the heart of the courtyard.

Around them were a mass of buildings; storage rooms, stables, and a tall standing keep, the heart of the castle. With sculpted masonry and statues, the keep was a magnificent sight.

A man stood just outside the doorway as Lara approached the main entrance of the keep. She curtsied before speaking.

"Pardon my ignorance, Sir, but my name is Lara Fergusson Moray, and I have come to see my father, William Fergusson. I was told that he had journeyed here several weeks ago. Do ye ken how I could find him?"

"Lady Moray," he said and bowed to her in return. "I am Godfrey, King Magnusson's chancellor. I am afraid yer father is away with the king. He shall return tomorrow. For now, I am sure Queen Isobel would not mind yer presence until he returns. And who do ye be?"

"My name is Bram MacKinnon, brother to Laird MacKinnon of the Highlands."

"Verra well. Follow me."

Bram kept a keen eye on his surroundings for any sign of danger as they walked into the great hall. Bram had never been inside a royal place. The walls were draped in luxurious tapestries, and sconces lit up the room. Instead of fresh rushes, the floor was made of polished wood, and behind the tapestries the walls were painted a soft cream color. Similar to a church, the windows were covered with figured stained glass and created a rainbow of colors from the sunlight shining through them. It felt too rich for his blood. He was better off in the Highlands.

At the head of a very long table sat a woman holding her bairn and a guard standing on each side of her. Seeing that she was dressed in a fine garment with jewels dangling across her neck, it took Bram only moments to realize that the woman holding the babe was none other than the Queen of Norway.

"Your Highness, may I present Lara Fergusson Moray, daughter of William Fergusson and her escort Bram MacKinnon."

"My lady, sir, I present to you Queen Isobel," the chancellor announced.

Her dark green eyes went directly to Lara and widened as if she had seen a ghost. Her face turned grim as she pursed her lips together.

"Fergusson?"

"Aye, my lady," Lara replied feeling the Queen's cold gaze.

"I wish to speak to the lass. Leave us. Both of you," Queen Isobel ordered, without taking her eyes off Lara. Suddenly, the room felt cold.

Before he could voice a dispute, the chancellor stood in front of Bram, blocking him from both the queen's and Lara's views. Leaving her was foolish and he would do no such thing. He was about to object when Lara looked over the chancellor's shoulder and said, "I will nay be too long Bram, I promise."

Lara looked back at the queen, whose sharp gaze bore down on her like a dagger. The queen continued to watch her until Bram and the chancellor left the room and closed the door.

Still holding the sleeping bairn, Queen Isobel asked, "You say William Fergusson is your father?"

"Aye, my Lady."

"That is a very clever story. But I do no' see why you had to lie to enter these gates. Were you sent here as a spy, or to help one of our enemies lay siege to our castle?"

The insult was overwhelming. Why would Lara lie about who she was? "William Fergusson is my father, yer Grace," Lara argued.

"I dinna know how that could be, lass, for William only has one child, a son. If you truly are his daughter, then may I ask who your mother is?"

"My mother was Elsa, but she died when I was ten and two, my Lady."

Queen Isobel continued to look at her in disbelief. "How old are ye?" she asked.

"Ten and seven."

Lara had no idea what to think of her questions, or where they would lead, but they caused the pit of her stomach to ache. Why would she lie? Why wouldn't her father mention that he had a daughter? It made no sense. Clearly, she did not trust Lara's claim to be a Fergusson. She wanted to run away from this moment, from this place; but she had little choice in the matter until she spoke with her father. She wished Bram had not been escorted out of the room. She needed his strength.

"If you are who you say you are, we will find out in due time. For now, you can stay in one of our guest rooms until William and my husband return. You will not be allowed to wander freely around the castle. If you need something, I will have one of my maids tend to it, and a guard to escort you when needed. I expect my husband to arrive in the early hours of the morning. At that time we will meet again." Speaking louder, she called out to a guard positioned just outside the door. "Take Lady Moray and her escort to the guest rooms on the third floor. Make sure Alba tends to their needs."

"Aye, my lady," he responded and escorted her out the door.

"Is everything alright? Are ye well?" Bram asked.

Lara shook her head, but looked back at the guard. She did not wish to speak in front of him. Bram wrapped an arm around her shoulders while they followed the guard up three flights of stairs. Once they reached the top floor, they walked down a corridor, lined with several closed doors. Eventually they reached the door at the end of the long hallway.

"This will be your room," the guard announced to Lara. "The next door down will be yours," he said, looking at Bram. "I will send Alba to your rooms with food and drink. There will be a guard posted at the end of the hallway if you are in need of something."

"Thank ye," Bram said, as the guard walked away, leaving them alone outside the bedchamber door.

Before she had time to think, Lara threw herself into Bram's arms sobbing. Bram held her close and walked with her inside the chamber before closing the door. Walking her to the bed, he helped her to sit down.

"What happened, lass? What did she say to upset ye?"

Through sniffles and tears, Lara replied, "The queen was just awful, and said the most wicked things. She called me a liar. She said that I could no' be my father's daughter. Why would she think I would lie about that?"

Bram frowned back at her, wishing he could take away her heartache and tears. "I dinna ken, lass."

"She said that my father and the king were away and will no' arrive here until the morning."

"Then we will wait. Dinna worry, lass. I will no' leave ye. We will figure this out together."

That declaration made Lara smile and begin to feel better. She knew that Bram would be by her side. In her whole life, no man, not even her own father, had shown as much compassion towards her as Bram had shown her in just one week.

Lara leaned her head against his big arm, and together they sat in silence, waiting for the maid to enter with their meal.

Isobel sat in her solar nursing her young daughter. Disturbed by her thoughts, she chose to take her meals in private, as she did not wish to be in the company of others.

Isobel did not know what to think of Lara's assertion. She had known the Fergusson clan since before she married her husband, Eric. William had been a member of Eric's army until he left for Scotland some twenty years ago with his wife Elsa, and John, who was just a bairn at the time.

She thought about her husband and their secret, and hoped that the decision he had made was the right choice, not just for them, but for all of Norway.

A loud rumble came from the door, waking the babe, who had fallen asleep in her arms. Over the bairn's loud cries, Isobel ordered the person to enter.

Godfrey stood in the doorway.

"My lady, you asked to see me?"

"Yes. Godfrey, as soon as my husband returns, I must speak to him. It is an urgent matter," she instructed the chancellor.

"Yes, my lady."

Isobel thought it was best to speak to her husband before speaking to William about the girl who occupied the guest room above. Eric knew William better than he knew himself, and if anyone had answers, it would be him. She'd never cared much for William, as he drank too much and had been known to use trickery in the past. She, herself, had reservations about his son John becoming king. If the truth were exposed, there would be an uproar, a mutiny the country had never seen. She thought to once again question her husband when he returned. But in the meantime, while he was away, she would keep her suspicions about the lass to herself.

Chapter 17

As night came, a cool breeze blew through the opened window. Lara went to sit by the fire as a shiver crawled down her spine. After their meal, Bram had retired to his room for the night to sleep, but Lara could do no such thing. She was too anxious to sit in one spot, let alone sleep. She had been pacing the room until her legs ached. Dawn could not come soon enough.

Lara could not stop herself from looking out the window after every sound she heard from outside. She felt a mix of emotions; anxiety, fear, loneliness. She was anxious for her father's arrival and afraid that Dermot would come, but the thoughts and feelings that weighed her down were those for the man who slept in the room on the other side of the stone wall.

Including the nights in the dungeon, this was the first night they had been apart in several weeks; it had been weeks since she had slept in a room by herself. It made her feel uncomfortable - the room felt too big. She wanted to ask the guard down the hall to move her to the room with the scullery maids so she wouldn't be alone. Remembering the queen's warning, though, she did not wish to anger her any more than she already had.

She stared at the stone wall and wondered what Bram was doing at that very moment. Was he tossing and turning from his nightmares, or was he also lying awake unable to sleep? After several long moments, she tiptoed to the door. Very quietly, she turned the latch and pulled the heavy wooden door open. Poking her head out, she looked down the hallway towards the staircase where the guard stood watch. The corridor was dark, and the light at the far end of the hallway was dim. In nothing but her white linen chemise, she stepped out into the corridor and lightly stepped down the hall towards Bram's room.

Gently, she tapped on the door three times, but no one answered. She waited a moment to see if he would answer, but still, no sound came from inside the room. Lara slowly turned the handle to the door and pushed it open. Inside, sparks of light danced along the walls from the low-burning embers in the hearth. She could see Bram's form lying on the bed turning his head from side to side. *Another nightmare.* Every night they'd been together he'd had them. As Lara crept further into the room, the floor boards creaked.

Bram was wakened out of his dream by a noise at the foot of his bed. This time, it was not the haunting nightmares he had been having the past sennight. He'd dreamt of Lara. In his dream, he was chained to the wall across the room from Lara and another man. The man had her pinned down on the floor, hurting her and trying to have his way with her while Bram was powerless to save her. Struggling against his chains, he'd used all of his strength to break free, but it was hopeless.

When he woke, his breathing was labored, and he could feel the sweat beading on his forehead. In the silence of the dark room, he could hear the faint sound of breathing and the wooden floor squeaking as if someone shifted their weight from one side to the other.

"Who goes there?" he called out to the intruder.

"Tis me," Lara answered back. "I'm sorry that I woke ye."

Bram sat up when he heard Lara's voice. His tired eyes blurred his vision, and it took a moment for him to focus. At first, he was unsure if he had really heard her in his room, or if it was her voice that had echoed to him through his dream.

However, real or imagined, the sound of her voice was like the calm before a storm.

"Lara? Are ye alright, lass? Did something happen?" he asked, concerned that he had slept through some unexpected event.

"Nay, nothing happened. I could no' sleep and I…I was lonely. I am no' used to sleeping alone anymore, and I thought that perhaps, if it were alright wit ye, I could sleep here on the floor."

Her soft-spoken words made Bram feel more vulnerable to his desires for her. How many nights had he wished for her to ask to sleep close to him? And how many of those nights did he suffer in agony wanting to hold her in his arms and kiss her sweet lips?

"Ye will no' be sleeping on the floor, lass."

"I cannae sleep wit' ye on the bed, and I would no' ask fer ye to sleep on the floor," she quickly replied.

"If it would make ye feel more comfortable, why dinna ye sleep here in my room and I will sleep in yer room. But I will stay here wit' ye until ye fall asleep, so that ye are no' alone."

Lara thought about his idea; it was a valid suggestion. She knew that they would not be allowed to share a room. If her father found out, she knew that all manner of hell would break loose. Nodding her head, Bram moved over to the other side of the bed. Quietly and uncomfortably, Bram and Lara lay side by side. Lara felt a warm sensation resonating through her.

"Thank ye," she said trying to mask the tension in her voice.

"Yer welcome," Bram replied rolling onto to his side facing away from her.

Under the covers, Lara could feel the heat radiating from his skin. She turned towards him; his bare back exposed to her made her thoughts run wild. What was the matter with her? She felt her nerves crawl under her skin and her breathing hitched. She longed for him to turn around and hold her, even though she wanted to resist. She pined for his attention and yearned for his kisses. The desire within her was almost so unbearable she wanted to scream. Overwhelmed with sensation, tears instantly filled her eyes.

Bram heard Lara shuffle on the bed and rolled to look at her. From the dying light of the embers, he could see the shine of her teary eyes.

"Oh lass. Dinna worry. Tomorrow yer father will be here, and everything will work out," he said, as he gathered her in his arms.

Lara snuggled herself deeper into his hold. Sucking in a quick breath of air, she looked up at him and gazed into his eyes. Bram placed a hand on her cheek and rubbed his thumb across her jawline. Sensing no resistance to his touch, he continued to run his fingers through her long hair stopping at the base of her neck. Scooping her hair to the side, he let it fall through his fingers leaving her neck exposed. Bringing his hand back to her cheek, he placed his fingers under her chin and lowered his head towards her, until he was but a breath away. Barely touching his lips to hers, he savored the moment and waited for her to push him away, but she didn't. Instead, to his surprise, Lara raised her head towards him, closing the space between them.

Bram's kiss was urgent and demanding. All thought and reason left Lara's mind. She felt her spirit lifted as if she soared through the heavens. His touch, his kiss, unlocked desires within her she never knew she had, or even thought possible. This, she knew, would change everything; but for that moment, she did not care. She did not care whether she angered her father, or if Dermot found her, for she felt the courage to face both of them.

Bram firmly pressed his tongue against her lips encouraging her to open. Once Lara submitted to him, Bram deepened the kiss. As Bram's hands vigorously moved up and down her back, he pressed her tighter against him, causing a flood of uncertain sensations. Lara could feel awareness of her body's need as she felt an aching desire in the most secret parts of her body.

As their lips pulled apart, they both gasped for air. Lara drew in a long and shaky breath. She did not want to fight her feelings any longer and she did not want to push him away. She welcomed his kisses, though she knew it was wrong of her to do so.

Before he lost all of his dignity and righteousness, Bram had to break the kiss. His need for her had become unnerving, and the swell of his groin had been urging him on, but he forced himself to stop. He would not tarnish her name or her honor. These feelings were a whole new experience for him. Was he not the man who just months ago bedded down with willing whores? Had he not been one to talk about marriage as if it was a fool's game? How did one lass change all of that? Bram never thought of himself as righteous or honorable when it came to women, but he would do right by Lara.

"The hour is late and ye need yer rest," he told her as he placed a gentle kiss on her forehead.

"Are ye leaving?"

Bram kissed her forehead, her cheeks, and her lips.

"Nay, lass," he smiled down at her. "I am no' leaving ye, but I must return to the other room before the sun rises and we are caught in bed together. I dinna want anyone to think that something had happened between us, as that would no' be good for either of us."

"Will ye come back in the morning?" Lara anxiously asked wanting him to be there by her side when her father arrived.

"Aye, lass. I will."

Lara's eyes fluttered closed, and she quickly faded into a deep sleep. When Bram was certain Lara was fast asleep, he rolled out of bed, snatched his tunic from the floor, and headed to the room down the hall for the remainder of the night. He was in awe of what had transpired between them, and looked forward to tomorrow, when he could kiss her again.

Chapter 18

A loud commotion outside the window woke Lara out of a deep sleep. She jumped out of bed and ran to the window to see what was occurring just outside. More than fifty horses came barreling across the drawbridge and emerged into the courtyard.

The horses were draped in red and blue royal trappings while their riders were dressed in armor. In the center of the assembly of riders, a large man with black hair stood out from the rest. He sat high upon his horse and wore fine furs around his wide shoulders. Next to him, sitting atop their horses, were John and heather. So anxious was she to see them, Lara could have leapt from the window.

She quickly turned and left the room, running down the hall to where Bram was sleeping. Without knocking, she burst through the door to announce her father's arrival, but the room was empty. The bed was made, and there showed no sign that anyone had even slept in the room. Lara's heart dropped in her chest. She worried if Bram had been caught wandering the hall while he was walking between the two rooms, or if he had left and headed back to Scotland. Lara refused to believe the latter, as he had made her a promise. He may have been a wretched Highlander, but she believed him to be honorable.

She quickly slipped her dress on over her chemise, then pulled on her boots, not even having the time or patience to tie the leather straps. She left the room running: down the hallway, then down the stairs into the great hall. In the great hall, a large crowd filled the room, making it impossible to find her brother and father amongst all of the people. Lara was short, and most of the men in the room seemed to be double her height and size. As she squeezed past them, she found her brother and father talking privately in the back corner.

"John, Father," Lara cried out and ran towards them.

John noticed Lara first as she bumped past a group of men trying to reach them. Giving her a smile, he held his arms out to the crying lass.

"Lara!" he said, as she fell into his embrace. "What are ye doing here?"

"I must talk to both of ye in private. It is of great importance," she said, looking at both her brother and her father.

William nervously looked about the room and grabbed onto Lara's arm, escorting her into an adjacent chamber. The room was small, with four chairs around a circular table. Hung on the walls were portraits of the Magnusson Royal family, and books were stacked high on shelves around the room. Lara was amazed; she had never seen so many books.

In a demanding and angered tone, her father asked, "Why are ye here, and where is yer husband?"

"He is no' here, Father. I traveled here wit' an escort."

Lara had never seen such anger in her father's eyes before. She tried to continue, but he immediately stopped her.

"Ye have nay business here. Ye will return to Scotland on the first boat."

"But Father, ye must listen."

"Nay, ye listen! I married ye off to Laird Moray. Ye are nay longer my responsibility. We have a contract with their clan fer this union," he yelled and slammed his fist on the table.

Lara's bottom lip trembled, and her eyes grew misty. Talking to him was useless. He truly had cast her to the wolves. But why? Why did he hate her so much? Lara ran out the door in tears, and John followed.

"Damnation, if that lass ruins everything I have worked for," William muttered to himself.

John caught up with Lara in the garden. She had been sitting on the bench, crying with her head in her hands. Slowly, he approached her, not wanting to frighten her.

"Lara. Ye can no' run away every time he yells at ye," he said, sitting down next to her and placing his hand on her shoulder for comfort.

"I dinna understand him, John. Why does he hate me?"

"I dinna ken. He is tough on me too. What are ye doing here?"

"Dermot…he is a treacherous mon, John. He lied about his wealth. He is nay richer than a lone peasant. English soldiers came to our keep, and when he could no' pay, he gave them me in exchange for his debt. I spent weeks in a dungeon, was treated cruelly. They barely fed me or allowed me to sleep." She sputtered, trying to catch her breath.

John's look of concern was etched on his face. "How did ye escape and travel this far all on yer own?"

"I killed the guard. And I have no' travelled alone. My escort is a Highland warrior. He is a verra brave and honorable mon."

"A Highlander!" John looked astonished.

"Aye. John, I can nay go back to Foley Castle. I believe Dermot may already ken I escaped the dungeon; he sent men to search fer me. I fear if he finds me, he will kill me. Please dinna let Father make me go back to him," Lara pleaded through tears.

"Lass, I am yer brother. I will protect ye. Have ye told anyone else this story since ye have been here?"

"Nay."

"Good. I dinna ken if ye ken this but many great things are happening. The King is dying. It is a secret even to his own men. Because his daughter Lady Margaret died many years ago, and his new babe is just a wee bairn, I have been chosen to be his successor. The only heir to the throne is his brother, and King Magnusson will do anything to keep him from the throne."

"But how can ye be king if ye are of nay royal blood?"

John wickedly smiled and explained, "Because we told his people that I am his cousin. My coronation is tomorrow evening. Once I am king, I promise ye that ye will have nothing to worry about again. Ye must tell nay one of this secret. Nay e'en yer Highland companion. Ye must promise me."

"Nay, of course, Brother."

Lara drew in a comforting deep breath. She knew that if Dermot did arrive, she had both Bram and now her brother to protect her. She smiled and gave her brother a bear-sized hug.

Bram mingled in the great hall with the crowd of men after he found Lara's room empty. He had checked on her in the wee hours of the morning, but she lay asleep, and he did not wish to wake her. Instead of returning to his own room, he had gone downstairs to break his fast. Before he knew it, alarms sounded announcing the king's arrival, and several dozen riders rode through the gates.

When Bram could not find Lara in her room, he assumed she had found her father and was somewhere in the castle speaking to him. He only hoped that her father would listen. From what Lara told him, he was not too sure the man could be trusted.

All night, Bram could think of nothing but the passionate kiss he'd shared with Lara. It was anything but innocent. When he felt her kiss him back, he knew that she wanted him as much as he wanted her, though she refused to admit it. Still, he needed to keep his feelings to himself for now. He had no idea what today would bring. Whether he would send her back to her husband or get the marriage annulled lay in the hands of her father. Bram knew that if there was an annulment, he would ask for her hand. But would she accept? Bram's palms began to sweat when the thought entered his mind. His chest tightened with both anticipation and anxiety.

The King of Norway came bursting through the tall double doors, greeting several of the men in the room. Bram had never met King Eric Magnusson, but had heard that the man was fierce in battle. He overheard a group of men talking about the King's recent campaign battling the Danish army and the success it had brought to his people.

King Eric was a tall man, with long, wild black hair and a pale complexion. He looked exactly as one would imagine a Norse Viking would. There was something particularly odd about him. He walked with a proud gait but seemed to favor his right leg over his left, and he appeared to be clutching onto his left arm. There was also something oddly familiar about him, though Bram had never seen the man before.

As a man experienced in battle and a warrior since childhood, Bram sensed that the King's injuries were far greater than he displayed. He knew how a man looked when trying to hide battle wounds. Bram observed the other men in the room. Not one of them seemed to have taken notice of the King's condition. Bram assumed that King Eric was either too proud or too stubborn to admit his health was declining.

King Eric raised a cloth to his lips and coughed profusely against it. Before he slipped it back into his pocket, Bram noticed the blood stain upon it. It became all too clear to him. The King wasn't just injured, he truly was dying. That much had not been a lie.

Bram walked around the courtyard, patiently waiting for Lara to return from speaking to her brother. A guard had informed him that the two of them had taken occupancy in the garden earlier.

"Bram," Lara called out, as she came running towards him from the garden gate.

Her smile and bright eyes made him wish he could take her into his arms and kiss her a thousand times, but in public they had to keep their distance.

"Bram, I worried ye had already left."

"Nay. I promised ye I would stay and make sure that ye were safe. Did ye talk wit' yer father?"

Lara's smiled was quickly replaced with a lowered brow a tightness about her lips

"Aye. He is angry that I came here, and demanded that I return to Scotland at once, but I dinna have to worry about that anymore. Nor do I have to worry about Dermot ever again."

"Why?"

"Tomorrow is my brother's coronation. When he is announced king, he promised to offer me protection within these walls. He promised that he would send word to our priest to have the marriage annulled. Isnae that wonderful news?" Lara asked grinning from ear to ear.

"Aye, lass. I am glad that all has worked out fer ye."

Bram's eyes saddened.

"What is the matter wit' ye? Are ye nay happy fer me?"

"Aye, lass. I am," he said, and it wasn't all a lie. Happiness was something he very much wanted for her, but he wanted to be the cause of it.

"What about ye? Now that I am safe, will ye be heading back to Scotland?"

"Most likely. I have planned to leave soon."

"Will ye at least stay for the coronation?"

Lara's pleading eyes were hard to resist. Bram pressed his palm against her soft cheek.

"Aye, lass I will."

For the remainder of the day, Bram stayed close to Lara's side, not wanting to miss any time he had left with her. They sat at one of the tables in the great hall with a few of the men from the village, drinking tankards of ale and sharing stories of battle. They talked and laughed until the wee hours of the night, as the servants prepared the castle for tomorrow's coronation. Hundreds of guests were expected to arrive.

Lara had spent the rest of the day avoiding contact with her father. She wanted to believe that John's talk with him about his plan would ease his mind. For when John became King, there would no longer be a need to continue the alliance with Clan Moray.

Chapter 19

"Ride faster, ye eejits," Dermot yelled to his men. They had been riding on Norse land for over an hour, and still had several more hours ahead of them. Traveling across the sea at night, they had arrived on the shores of Norway just before the sun crested the horizon.

Dermot was determined to get to Bergen as quick as possible and get his wife back. He had kept the ruse of the mournful husband for long enough, but when word came that Lara had somehow managed to escape her prison, he feared that the rights to her dowry and treasure would be taken from him. His anger grew the more he thought about the ungrateful wench. How dare she deny what belonged to him; both her treasure and her body! She was his wife, and she would love, obey, and honor him with her very last breath. Dermot wickedly chuckled to himself at the thought of being the cause of that last breath.

Never had he imagined settling for such a defiant lass. If it were not for his greed and taste for wealth, he would have denied his father's order to marry her. Dermot wished to just kill her and not waste his time or strength prancing around as if he missed his bride. He was rather proud of himself for his clever idea to allow the English to take her instead of having to deal with her himself; it was quite convenient, actually, that they arrived when they had.

Dermot knew that if Lara had already arrived in Bergen, he would once again need to act as if she had been kidnapped, as everyone else in his clan had. His biggest concern was that Lara could somehow prove or convince her father that their marriage had not yet been consummated. That one minor detail caused their union to hang in the balance. According to their laws, if the marriage had not been consummated within a fortnight, the contract of union was automatically annulled, though there were always exceptions. Using the excuse that she had been kidnapped was one of those exceptions that he was certain the priest would sanction.

"My Laird, once we find yer runaway bride, will we be returning directly to Foley?" one of his men asked.

"Aye, we will no' waste another minute on this Godforsaken land. I dislike these Vikings as much as I do the French and the English," he replied. Both he and his guard laughed at his remark. "I wish to retrieve me bonny wife and return home."

Dermot had to be cautious of revealing his motives for rescuing his wife. With only a few short hours left, Dermot rehearsed the words needed to be said to ensure possession of his bride.

Sitting in a chair next to the side of her bed, Bram watched Lara as she slept. Her black hair sprawled out across her pillow, and the covers tightly snuggled around her. After too many shots of whiskey she had fallen into a coma-like sleep. With only a solitary candle lit, he studied her face, wanting to remember every curves and shape. She truly was the most beautiful lass in all of Scotland, and now that she was on Norse lands, all of Norway as well.

Brushing a wisp of hair away from her face, he whispered, "Lara, I dinna ken why I do' nay have the courage to tell ye this, but the last few days ye have brought forth a light inside of me I ne'er ken existed. Ye saved me from the darkness that night, like the angel of mercy. When I am no' with ye, I feel as if part of me is lost; and when I see yer smile, I am whole again. I would sacrifice all I have, all I am fer ye."

Bram sat back against the back of the chair and continued to watch her sleep until the sky began to lighten and rays of orange could be seen transcending over the vista of mountains and valleys.

Lara woke with a pounding headache. Never had she drank so much ale and whiskey, but as soon as she emptied her cup, Bram, her brother and the other men filled it cup back to the rim. They were celebrating John's last night as a vassal.

Wanting to show that a lass could keep up with a man, she did not back down from the challenge. Over the night, the group of them challenged themselves into a drinking contest, which ended very badly for her. Lara had spent the night throwing up in the privy while Bram once again held her hair. The last thing she recalled was Bram carrying her up to her room and laying her on the bed. After that, she had passed out.

With her head pounding, every sound made her feel as if she stood next to the church bells as they rang in her ears. Lara took the pillow and placed it over her head to drown out the noise. It seemed to be getting louder and louder. Even the light from the window seemed to burn her eyes. Lara rolled over, feeling the urge to empty her stomach, but the result was only dry-heaves.

"Ye will be wanting to drink this, lass," Lara heard Bram say from somewhere in the corner of the room.

Lara sat up, her hair hanging over her face like the long thin leaves and branches of a willow tree. Brushing her hair to the side, she slowly opened her eyes and saw a blurry image of Bram standing next to her bed holding onto a mug.

"What is it?" her voice hoarse and scratchy, as if she had spent the entire night yelling.

"Tis ale."

"Oh nay," Lara said and fell backwards, landing on the bed, then covering her head with the blanket. The idea of drinking any liquor made her stomach cringe. She swore that she would never again drink any substance that would cause her head to spin and stomach to roll. Bram laughed out loud.

"Lass, I promise, it will only make ye feel better."

Under the blanket, she mumbled, "How can drinking poison make me better?"

"Just drink it, ye stubborn lass."

188

Lara popped her head out from the covers and sat up. With shaky hands, she reached for the mug and drank the cold ale. Soon, her stomach settled and the pounding lessened. Bram sat on the chair next to her bed with an all-too-confident grin on his face. The look aggravated Lara, and if she felt up to par, she would have gladly dragged him out to the loch and drowned him.

"Feel better?" he asked, still grinning.

Lara took in a sharp breath and released it hastily, loud enough for Bram to hear her snort in response to his comment. She did not like the enjoyment he got out of proving her wrong all the time. Bram was very much like her brother, in the sense that he often teased her in a playful way, but the feelings she had for him where more than brotherly love, and the kiss they shared told her that the care he had for her was just as strong. A wave of sadness went over her like a dark cloud. Today was their last day together, and what a journey it had been. She knew in her heart that she would never forget her Highland warrior.

Looking at his tousled hair and clothes, Lara realized that he had not changed.

"Did ye sleep here last night, in the chair?" she asked.

"Aye I did. I wanted to be close in case ye fell ill again." Bram stood and raked his fingers through his hair. "The coronation is to start when the sun is at its highest in the sky. Ye should get dressed," he suggested.

"Where are ye going?"

Bram could hear a pitch of sadness in her voice.

"I need to gather my things and prepare my horse for my journey back to the port. My boat leaves later this evening and I do no' wish to miss it. I will leave ye now to dress, my lady," he replied and walked towards the door.

As Bram grabbed the handle, he felt his heart shatter into a million tiny pieces. While watching Lara sleep, he'd whispered a promise to her to not steal anymore kisses, or speak words of love and devotion. Her brother had vowed to protect her, and as king, he had greater power than Bram ever would. She would be safe among family. Bram opened the door and walked out into the corridor. It was time to go home.

Chapter 20

Visitors from near and far gathered in the bailey and the courtyard as they waited for the coronation to commence. While farmers, smiths, and other commoners waited for the new king to present himself on the castle's balcony, the Lords, Earls, and other nobility waited to be seated in the cathedral. Charging through the gates, Dermot and his men searched for William Fergusson or some sign of Lara.

Donning a borrowed dress that the maids had brought her, Lara finished readying herself by braiding her long black hair, intrinsically linking each braid starting at the crown of her head and allowing the length of it to flow down her back. The dress she wore was dark burgundy and reminded her of a bright-colored rose when it first started to bloom. The v-shaped neckline was stitched with gold thread, and matched the golden slippers peeking out from the skirt.

As sister to the king, Lara assumed that she would take her place by her brother's side during the ceremony, whether her father agreed with it or not. With her brother's new position, she no longer felt she needed to fear her father. It was not the first time she had angered him in her seventeen years, nor would it be the last. In the past, his lectures had been repetitive, but usually his anger subsided, and he moved on, pointing out other things Lara had said or done to upset him. The only liberty she had was permission to move about the castle and come and go as she pleased.

As Lara made her way from the great hall to the courtyard and into the mass of visitors, she froze at the sight in front of her. Suddenly, as if caught in a storm, Lara spun around, pushing past the crowd to shield herself from the group of kilted men displaying Clan Moray insignia and colors.

"He's here," she whispered to herself, her hands trembling.

Scanning the courtyard, she looked for Bram and John to seek protection, but neither of them could be found among the men. She thought to blend in with a group of women who were talking amongst themselves along the castle wall and scurried over to them.

From the corner of her eye, she saw Dermot forcefully grab the shoulder of every black-haired lass in the courtyard, turning them to face him as if he expected to see Lara's silvery eyes staring back. The women squealed at his assault, which quickly angered their male escorts. Commotion stirred and voices were raised.

"What is the meaning of this?" a loud, booming voice hollered over the crowd.

The people standing in the courtyard became stone silent and all eyes fell on the man standing at the top of the stairs. He was tall with black shaggy hair and dressed in formal attire. Lara watched as the group of people bowed in unison. Instinctively, she did the same. *The King!*

Lara knew that the King had returned from his journey with her father and brother, but since his arrival, he had been locked away in his library and solar attending business. Now, with the arrival of distant travelers, here to celebrate, he finally made his presence known.

"My apologies, my Lord. I believe Laird Dermot has traveled here to discuss an issue wit' me. I apologize for the disturbance his presence has caused," William explained, as he walked towards Dermot from the other end of the courtyard.

Lara, still hidden behind the group of women, watched her father as he went to stand next to Dermot and whisper something to him.

"I do no' like disruptions, William. See that the situation is dealt with," Eric replied, and turned to go back inside the castle.

William nodded his head towards the gates, indicating to Dermot that he wished to speak to him in private. At least, that was Lara's, interpretation as the two men walked towards the battlement and disappeared under the portcullis. She spotted John standing near the stables; he too had seen the embarrassing display, and ran after them. Lara worried what her brother and father would say. For now, her fate rested in their hands.

"What are ye doing here?" William asked.

"I thought my wife had been kidnapped. Should I no' be concerned about my estranged wife?"

William looked at him suspiciously.

"I find that hard to believe, as she came here by her own free will and wit an escort. A Highlander. Ye have no' proved yerself truthful or trustworthy. And ye cannae e'en protect and keep track of yer own wife. She is nay more than a lass wit' her head in the clouds. How did ye let her escape the castle grounds?"

Dermot ground his teeth before speaking.

"She is a disobedient and defiant wench. I gave her every freedom, more than she deserved, and still she denied me. When no one could find her, I assumed that she was either kidnapped or the foolish lass had run away. I followed her trail to Stearns, but when I reached the castle I learned that she had traveled here to find ye. As fer her Highland friend, I dinna ken who he is, but I can assure ye that I will find him and bury him. "

"And why do ye suppose she would have done that?"

"She dinna tell ye?"

"Nay," William barked.

Dermot considered his answer. Perhaps the lass was too afraid to tell her father what had really happened. He thought to rectify the matter and retrieve his wife before all was lost to him.

"My Laird, there is something ye should ken which should be of great importance to ye. We have no' consummated the marriage. I have tried to be tender wit' the lass, but she is as stubborn as a horse. Ye do ken what this means, aye?"

"Aye. If ye dinna consummate it, the union between our clans is null and void," William said in a gruff tone, more angry with his daughter than anything.

"Aye. That is why I have come here to collect my wife. If the neighboring clans learn we hold nay truce, they will rebel and war will break out. The lass has caused more trouble than she kens," Dermot reminded him.

Now, he had no choice but to return Lara to him.

"I agree wit' ye. I will fetch her, and ye will take her on the first boat back to Scotland. I trust that ye can manage no' losing her again?"

"Aye, of course, my Laird."

William walked back inside the courtyard and searched for Lara. John stayed behind and glowered at Dermot. Lara had run up the stairs to the top of the curtain wall and watched the scene below, though she could not hear the conversation they were having.

"Why are ye really here? I ken it is no' fer Lara."

"As ye must ken, besides my insolent bride, I have no' received the other half of her dowry. Yer father promised me a treasure worth its weight in gold. And I expect to claim it."

John stared at him with icy blue eyes. Taking a step forward, he whispered, "I ken the truth. I ken what ye did."

Dermot held his breath, feeling threatened when John exposed his secret. As John continued to talk in his ear, Dermot, with precision and stealth, slid his dagger out of its sheath along his belt and slipped it into the sleeve of his tunic. Over time, the words John spoke were hazy and mumbled. With his mind focused on his surroundings, all Dermot could hear was the sound of his blood rushing and heart pounding in his ears. Each breath and exhale became louder and more distinct. Anger boiled in his veins when John spoke his last words.

As fast as a lightning bolt strikes the ground, Dermot raised his dagger to John and lurched towards him. Within moments, the two of them were wrestling on the ground. John twisted from side to side, avoiding the dagger held in Dermot's hand. Lara panicked and called out for help, but the commotion in the courtyard was so loud that no one heard her cries. Even the villagers outside the gates were too distracted to notice what was occurring.

John successfully plunged Dermot's own dagger through his heart. The color drained from Dermot's face, and the irises of his eyes grew dark. Dermot staggered back, and with both hands pulled the dagger out of his chest. Blood seeped out of the side of his mouth. He took one step, then another, before crashing down onto the ground. His cold and lifeless body doubled over and stiffened. Lara's panic caused her lungs to feel as if all of the air had escaped her, making it difficult to breathe. Through glistening eyes, Lara looked at John. He was standing over the dead man's body. Lara ran down the steps to join him. Staggering towards her, John wrapped his arms around her. He escorted her away from the view of Dermot's corpse.

"Go to yer room. I will meet ye there soon. Dinna worry, dear sister, I promise ye everything will be alright," John said, smiling down at her.

By the time Bram reached the front gates, a crowd had gathered around a lifeless body lying on the ground. Blood oozed from his chest. Bram recognized his Highland colors and assumed that the man lying dead on the ground was none other than Laird Moray, but questions raced in his mind about who had killed him. Had Lara taken another man's life? Had Dermot attacked her, hurt her? Dashing through the gates, he searched for Lara, but ran into her brother, John, instead.

"Where is Lara? Is she alright? Is she hurt?" Bram asked, fearful of the man's response.

"Nay, she is fine. She is waiting in her room for my return."

"Thank ye," Bram said, and dashed up the stairs towards Lara's room.

Chapter 21

"Something is amiss, husband, and it has to do with that lass." Queen Isobel spoke elegantly and her tone was smooth and soft as a gentle breeze.

"What girl?" Eric asked, as he rummaged through a stack of papers on his desk.

Isobel glided across the solar and placed her hand gently on her husband's, lowering the papers in his hand from his view.

"Heaven sakes, Eric. Why is it that you only hear half of what I tell you?"

Eric breathed in deeply and set the papers back down onto the table. Settling back into his chair, he looked at her, giving her his full attention.

"I do listen to you, you just happen to talk when I am busy, or eating, or sleeping, or…"

Eric snickered at the unamused look displayed on Isobel's face as she stood with arms crossed and foot tapping on the floor. "I am listening to you now, my love. Now, what were you trying to tell me?" he asked, as he reached out for his wife and pulled her down to sit in his lap.

Isobel wrapped her arms around his wide shoulders and continued. "As I was saying, something is going on and it has to do wit' that lass. That man who was killed at the gate, they say he was her husband. If William invited enemies or trouble into our midst, especially now…"

"I will talk to William and John, and whoever this lass is," Eric said cutting her off.

"Thank you."

Eric helped Isobel down from his lap and stood. Walking to the door, he opened it and summoned his guard.

"Gather William and the lass who is staying in the guest rooms upstairs, and meet me in the library."

"Yes, my Lord," the guard replied.

Eric would take care of this mess once and for all.

Lara sat on the edge of her bed, her hands shaking and mind spinning. Dermot was dead. Lara felt a sense of relief and freedom, as if a weight had been lifted from her shoulders. She was overjoyed. No longer was she bound to a loveless marriage. No longer did she have to fear him and what he would have done to her. No longer was she forced to bare his children, or be forced into warming his bed. She was a widow and free. Falling back onto the bed, she spread her arms out wide and breathed.

A soft knock came from the door. Sitting up quickly, she hurried to the door. Opening it, she smiled widely at Bram, who was standing in the corridor. Today, of all days, he looked rather handsome, shedding his dirty brown shirt and worn-out kilt for a clean white tunic and a pair of dark brown trews. With her new sense of freedom, she felt the walls she'd erected around her heart soften. Now there were no more reasons or excuses for pushing him away. Looking at him now, a flood of emotions began to overwhelm her.

"Are ye alright?" he asked.

"Aye. I am more than alright. Come in. I have so much to tell ye," she boasted, grabbing his hand and dragging him inside the chamber.

Sitting down in opposite chairs next to the hearth, Lara retold the story of what had happened between John and Dermot. She told him everything except what truly mattered - how she felt towards him.

"I have word that the boat for Scotland is leaving earlier than scheduled. So I have come to apologize that I have to break my promise. I will no' be here to attend the coronation.

Bram did not want to leave, though he knew it was time. He had fulfilled his promise, and every journey had to come to an end. Standing up, he quietly walked towards her. Leaning down, he grabbed her hand and placed a soft kiss on the back of it.

"It has been a true pleasure, my lady," he said as he lowered her hand and started towards the door. As he opened it, he heard Lara call out to him.

"Bram," Lara's voice trembled as she looked at him with desperate need.

Bram turned back to face her. "Aye."

"I…I dinna want ye to go," she whispered, staring into his eyes.

Bram could see the sadness in her eyes and a frown forming on her face. His heart skipped a beat. Hearing those words was all it took to change his mind. They were all he wanted to hear.

Slamming the door shut, he ran back to her. With great urgency, he grabbed her, pulling her into his arms, and tightly pressing her body against his. Lowering his lips, he kissed her firmly, with fervor, filled with want and need. Her lips were moist and tasted as sweet as nectar. He couldn't seem to get enough of her. He wanted to touch her; to feel her bare skin against his.

Bram was completely lost in the moment. Had he been another man, he would have ripped the dress right off her and taken her right then and there. He kissed her again and again, rubbing his hands wildly through her hair and down the expanse of her back, keeping her body against his so that there was no distance between them.

This was not meant to be a sweet and gentle kiss. This kiss was meant to ravish her, to breathe all of her in; her heart, her body, her soul. He kissed her as if his life depended on every touch, every breath; and when she pressed her body closer to his and deepened the kiss, he felt as if he was about to come completely undone. Emotions exploded through every chamber of his heart and each corner of his mind. In the back of his throat, he growled as his body ached with need. She was his, always and forever.

Bram's kiss caused Lara to become feverish. With each kiss, her desire and passion built higher than she had ever experienced or imagined. Sucking in sharp breaths of air, she felt as if she was about to swoon, but his grip kept her upright as she melted into him. She had been holding back for so long that this release of emotion and desire freed her from the inner torment she felt. She wanted Bram, all of him.

As they interlocked their fingers, Lara slowly started to calm herself as if she was descending from an imaginary summit.

"I ne'er want ye to leave," she whispered against his lips.

With her eyes still closed, she rubbed her cheek against his stubble and breathed him in. Bram loosened his embrace just enough to smile down at her. Raising his hand, he gently rubbed the side of her cheek. Lara's eyes were misty; not from sadness or anger, but from a sort of bliss she had never known. Reminiscing over the past few weeks, she knew her feelings were as certain as the moon and the stars that hung in the heavens. She loved him with her whole heart.

Startled by a loud pounding at the door, Lara was swept back into reality and jumped out of Bram's embrace. Heaven knew what would happen if her father came upon them, only hours after the death of her husband, bastard though he was. Trying to gain composure, Lara patted down her hair and straightened her dress on her shoulders. With a deep breath, she opened the door.

"My lady, you have been summoned to meet in the library," one of the royal guards informed.

"Summoned? By whom?"

"King Magnusson, my lady."

Why would the king want to see her? She held no title or land and was no one of importance. Nervously, she looked back at Bram. Biting her bottom lip, Lara followed the guard down the long hallway, with Bram following closely behind.

Eric stood next to the windowsill, staring out into the valley below. Heated by his discussion with William, he was convinced that William had lied. His story did not make any sense and was full of holes, as if he purposely meant to keep out important details. Eric may have been old and his memory had been fading from time to time since his illness, but he was not daft enough to overlook such. He needed to be able to trust William and his son.

His decision to fabricate the relationship of John as his cousin's son, allowing him to take the throne, had not come easy. But his hatred for his brother made the decision vital for his people and all of Norway. His brother did not support the war with Denmark, which was critical for Norway to maintain political power. He feared that if his brother became king, Norway would fall into the hands of either the English or the French.

William sat quietly across the room from where Eric was standing. Both of them waited for Lara to arrive. William tried to speak to defend himself, and tried to convince him that his daughter was daft and did not know how to present herself in front of royalty, but Eric would hear none of it. He would meet the lass and calm his wife's worry.

Chapter 22

Standing in front of the tall wooden door, Lara swallowed hard. It was nerve-wracking enough having to speak to the queen, but speaking to the King created an entirely different whirl of emotions. The doors to the library were carved with tiny spiral designs, and looked more like a work of art than just a door. Lara thought that even the handle was too fancy for such a simple object. Nervously, she grabbed onto Bram's hand, squeezing it tightly. Bram returned the grip with equal pressure.

"Ye will be alright," Bram said, as he placed a soft kiss to her forehead.

All Lara could do was smile. She had never been so nervous in her life. As the guard turned the handle, he pushed the door inward. The bright light from the room lit the dark corridor. Inside, Lara could see her father with King Magnusson, who was standing by the window with his back towards her.

Dropping Bram's hand before her father could see their display of affection, Lara slowly crept inside the room. As she stood in the center of the room, the guard excused himself and closed the door behind him. Lara looked over at her father. Seeing the anger painted on his face, Lara looked down, feeling like the ungrateful daughter she had been over the past two days. She had openly dishonored and defied him, and knew that her actions could have severe consequences.

Lara did not realize what she had done by coming here. It was because of her that Dermot had followed her here, and it was because of her that he was dead. What made matters worse was that she brought dishonor to her family, and was sure that the king would punish her and her father for her disobedience. She could do only one thing - ask King Magnusson to spare her family and her family's name, and she would accept whatever punishment he saw fit.

"Yer majesty, my Lord. It is me that ye have quarrel wit, no' my father or my brother. Laird Moray came here fer me, and I alone am responsible fer his actions here today. Fer that I know that I must be punished," Lara said bowing to him.

Staring down at the floor, she did not dare raise her gaze, for doing so would show as much insult as if she were to tell the King he smelled of horse dung.

Eric kept his eyes fixed on the scenery below his window. He was taken aback by the girl's words. Never would he have thought that William would have raised such an outspoken daughter. He took a sip of his whiskey and turned to face the bold lass standing in the middle of the room.

At the sight of her, he felt as if his heart stopped beating. His breath seized. Eric's reaction caused him to loosen his grip on his tankard of whiskey. As if the room stood still, the mug crashed onto the floor and shattered. The sound of tiny fragments scattering across the wooden floor, echoed throughout the room. In the pit of his stomach, he felt an overwhelming sense of anger and sadness colliding within him like an angry storm. He felt cold, yet began to sweat profusely, and suddenly found it hard to breathe.

In a trembling voice, he murmured, "Margaret? But you're dead!"

"Nay, my Lord, my name is Lara Fergusson. I mean, Lara Moray," Lara quickly corrected him, though curious why he would believe she was his dead daughter.

Eric turned and looked at William. Lara did not mistake the look in his eyes. She could have sworn they turned as black as coal. Lara believed that his building anger was so great that his eyes could have turned burning red while smoke exhaled from his nostrils like a mighty dragon. But rather than a dragon, this was a beast of another kind. A tormented man.

"What sort of black magic is this?" Eric questioned as he stood towering over William.

William sat quiet and turned his head from Eric. Grabbing his collar, Eric lifted him from his chair and dragged him across the floor until he was pinned up against the wall. Lara gasped as her father was attacked.

"Who is she?" Eric asked, as he pressed his hand tighter around William's throat. "Answer me!" Eric roared.

Gasping for air, William choked out, "Margaret's daughter."

Eric stood still for a moment, soaking in what William had just said.

"Liar! Margaret's children were all stillborn. Only Maid Margaret survived past infancy."

William coughed as he struggled to breath, "Nay. The lads were stillborn. The lass survived. Ye were so blind and foolish ye dinna deserve her. I loved Margaret. And if ye were nay in the way, she would have run off wit' me to Scotland, no' her sister Elsa. Once Margaret found out she was wit' child, she refused to leave ye. It was because of her," he choked out. "Lara was the reason why Margaret stayed wit' ye. I could nay have Margaret, so I took from ye what ye held most dear. Yer child."

"Why? Why would you raise her as your own?"

"Because I knew ye would need an heir. I never thought ye would find out about her."

"My throne! You did all of this because you were after my throne," Eric stated, acknowledging William's true purpose for offering John as his vassal.

Eric then turned to Lara. Feeling overwhelmed with pity for her, he realized that she too had been lied to. He could not imagine what the lass was feeling or thinking. All he knew was that she was his daughter, and would make William pay for what he had done to them both.

Lara shook her head. "It can nay be true," she whispered so quietly that only she could hear. Lara wanted to cover her ears; she could not stand to hear any more of it. Her own family had betrayed her. Her father, her mother. She only wondered if John also knew the truth, or if he too had been just a pawn in this game.

"William Fergusson," Eric growled, "You have committed treason and kidnapping and are to be condemned to death. By sunset tomorrow you will be hanged by the neck until life has been taken from you. May God save your wicked soul, for ye are bound for hell!"

Lara stood stone silent for several moments as the guards carried her father out of the room. She felt as if her whole world had spun out of control. Everything had been a lie. What was she to do now? With teary eyes she glanced up to the king, her father. She could feel the weight of his stare. His eyes were the same silvery grey as hers, and he too had the raven-black hair that matched her own. It all made sense. She never questioned why she looked so different from her mother and father, both of whom had bright red hair. But it was all because her father - or the man she thought to be her father - had kidnapped her from her real parents. Had she known, had there been any clue, she would have... Lara's mind went blank. In truth, she didn't know what she would have done.

Without a word, Lara turned and ran out the door. Running past the guard and up the flight of stairs, she ran into John and Bram, who were sitting on the top step drinking a tankard of ale. Noticing her distress, Bram quickly stood and wrapped his arms around her before sitting down next to her on the top step.

"I heard what happened to yer father. Are ye alright?"

Lara said nothing, but shook her head. She was anything but alright. He was he only thing in her life that was real.

"I swear to ye, I dinna ken," John said, lifting her chin to look at him. "How,for all this time, did he and mother keep that secret from us?"

"I dinna ken. Oh, Brother, it was all our father's doing. He lied to everyone. The King has sentenced him to death."

"I should have known. I am sorry, Lara. I should have protected you better. I should have been a better brother. He committed many crimes, and he deserves what is coming to him. His greed almost destroyed everything. He is a vicious mon, Lara. Do no' pity him."

"The treasure!" Lara exclaimed, and backed out of Bram's embrace.

"What?" John curiously asked.

Suddenly, Lara began to pace back and forth murmuring to herself.

"It all makes sense. There was ne'er any treasure. Dinna ye see? It was me, all along. I am the treasure he received from the Norse King. It was me! That is why nay one had ever seen it. It was right before their eyes."

Bram looked at Lara thoughtfully. Perhaps there was justice in the world. The treasure was not a chest of gold, as Dermot had believed. It was something more precious than any amount of coin or jewels. It was a beautiful, black-haired bairn with sterling grey eyes, the heiress to the Norwegian throne. Dermot had held the treasure, had unknowingly thrown it away, and then had died trying to get it back, still not realizing the truth of what he sought.

John's face turned grim. "I want to see him."

"Ye cannae see him. The king had him escorted to the dungeon. He said that father… William… was to hang by sunset tomorrow," Lara cried out.

"Then I will ask the king myself," John said, as he stood and began walking down the hall.

Lara ran to his side.

"What about yer coronation?"

"It will have to wait."

"I would like to join ye," she asked.

"Are ye sure ye want to do that, lass?" Bram asked.

"Aye. I must do this. I need to do this," she responded.

The three of them walked down to the library. The door was open and there was no guard in sight. Inside, Eric was sitting at his desk, with Queen Isobel by his side. He looked up when John stepped inside the wooden door frame.

"Yes?" Eric said looking back and forth between them.

"Yer majesty. I wish to see my father. I want to hear from his own lips what he has done, to me, to my sister," John asked in a sincere tone.

"Please," Lara asked, stepping within view of the king.

Eric's heart softened looking into Lara's eyes. She looked so much like her mother. It had been almost ten years since his wife Margaret had passed. The good Lord had taken her the day their daughter Maid Margaret was born. Eric had thought that when the Lord took Maid Margaret home with him to heaven that the Lord was punishing him. He'd repented his sins every sermon, once a week during the holy day, though he feared God could not hear him. But now, here, standing in front of him, was proof that the Lord had listened to his prayers. No longer did he feel like Job, as the priest had taught him.

"I will grant you permission, but the visit will be supervised, and you will no' go alone."

John bowed. "Thank ye."

Looking back at Lara, he said, "Had I known, I would have…" but Lara stopped him before he could finish.

"I know ye would have."

Offering him a sincere smile, he sat up and hugged Lara in a warm fatherly embrace. Even though she had only known him for one day, she knew that he loved her as much as a father could ever love a daughter. As for William, the man who'd raised her and her brother John, she did not know what was to come of him as his fate rested in the king's hands.

"My Lord, I hope you still consider accepting John as yer vassal. He is a good man, and will make a great king. Do no' punish him fer our… I mean, fer his father's doings."

"As you are my daughter, I will consider your request."

As Lara and John walked out into the hallway, Eric clenched his fists so tightly that he could have broken the bones of his fingers. With built up anger, he punched the stone wall behind his desk. He felt as if he could destroy everything in the room. Isobel cautiously stepped towards him.

"When I first saw her, I knew. She looks so much like you and Margaret."

Eric turned away from her. He could not bear to be reminded of the truth. How could he have a daughter of ten and seven? How could he have been so foolish in trusting William? The man he befriended. The man he trusted. The man deserved to die for what he had done.

"Go to her, Eric. You must speak to her."

"She doesn't know me. She doesn't even know who she is," he snapped.

"Give her time, Eric. She has been through much, and it will take time for her heart to heal. But you can start with today. Go to her," Isobel encouraged him.

"I don't know what to say."

Isobel gave him a soft smile, and gently pressed her hand to his shoulder.

"You have given the greatest of speeches before battle to your men, inspired your men to follow you. I am sure that when the time comes, you will know what to say. Say what is in your heart, my love, for no truer words can be spoken."

Chapter 23

Standing at the dungeon door gave Lara shivers down her spine. Haunting memories of a dark cell she had once endured caused the tiny hairs on her arm to stand on end. She would demand that William speak the truth and she would show him no mercy and have no pity for him.

John pushed his way into the dungeon and rushed over to the bars that imprisoned his father.

"Ye traitor," John said, and spit into the man's face.

William lowered his head, but kept his eyes firmly on John. Wiping the spit off his face, he replied in a cold tone, "I did it fer ye, ye eejit, ye fool. Ye would have been nothing if it were no fer me. I gave ye everything."

"I never wanted it," John growled.

Lara stepped up to the bars next to John. She had so many questions she wanted to ask, but she already knew the answers. She looked into his heartless eyes. They held no emotion, no regret, no sadness, and no fear. It was then that she knew he'd never loved her. Lara met his gaze, and for several long moments just stared at the bastard, silent and motionless. He was not worth the wrath of her words, nor did he deserve the dignity of explaining himself. She wanted him to know that from this day forth she would never think of him again. She would not mourn his death or pray for his soul. Souls like his did not belong in the glory of heaven. Lara turned and walked back out the door of the dungeon and back into the hallway.

"'Twas a brave thing ye done, lass," Bram said, walking up behind her.

"I am just glad that it is over."

Bram placed his hands against Lara's cheeks. As he bent down to kiss her John interrupted them.

"Well, if ye two are quite finished, we have a coronation to attend, aye?" John boasted.

Lara and Bram laughed at his enthusiasm.

The church held more than one hundred attendees. Everyone was dressed in their finest attire and sat quietly in the pews of the massive church. The nave was full of people, and the aisles were beautifully decorated with flowers of all kinds. The priest stood before the altar dressed in a white robe with a golden girdle tied around his waist. Around his shoulders was a red and gold stole with images of the cross stitched on each end. His headwear was also decorated in jewels, with gold trim around the base. Lara thought it looked very much like the crown that King Eric had worn. The King, who stood next to him at the altar, was draped in a massive fur cloak. With his sword by his side, he stepped up to stand next to the humble priest. John knelt before them. Eric held out his sword and gently tapped each of John's shoulders as the priest spoke words in Latin which Lara had trouble understanding. Thankfully, Bram translated the words for her by whispering in her ear.

The words the priest spoke sounded more like a sonnet or a poem, and even though she did not understand the words, they sounded beautiful and majestic. After the priest had finished, he draped a green stole over John's shoulders. He then, with both hands, lifted a jewel-encrusted gold crown that was resting on a red velvet pillow and slowly placed it on the top of John's head.

After the deed was done, the priest announced John as Norway's new young king. Lara knew that until the death of King Eric that John would not exist as sole king just yet, but the co-title would give him most of the same rights and privileges. John had told Lara in the garden that once he became king, King Eric's condition would be publicly announced to his people and John would then have full rights to the throne.

The very thought of Eric's illness saddened Lara. She knew that they had little time together before his health truly declined. Having not known he was her real father until now, she did not want to miss any opportunity to get to know him. She had so many questions about who her family was and where she had come from.

The ceremony went on for most of the afternoon and into the evening hours, followed by a grand feast in the gathering room. Bram sat next to Lara on the dais at the high table, along with King Eric, Queen Isobel, and John. Never had he felt so out of place and uncomfortable. He was a Highland warrior, and here he was sitting in front of fine linens and fancy tableware. This was nothing like Dunakin. At home they had nice things, but nothing to this extreme.

During the meal, Bram and John talked about uniting the Highland Clans and other politics, but his mind never left Lara. Underneath the table, he slipped his hand into hers. Rubbing his thumb over her knuckles, he stirred, wanting to touch more of her. He prayed that this night would end soon so that he could be alone with her. After this evening, he would ask for Lara to be his wife, and together they could return to the Highlands.

The corners of his mouth twitched at the thought of what his brother Rory and cousin Ewan would think of him as a married man. Had someone told him that one day he would find the love of his life and marry he would have told that person that he would rather roll 'round in cow dung than be tied down to only one woman. Thankfully, he'd never made that bet.

"It is good fortune that my sister found ye and brought ye here. I have a proposition for ye. I want ye to stay here and lead my army," John graciously offered.

"That is verra generous of ye, My Lord, but my place is home among my clansmen."

"We are among friends; ye can call me John. Come, join me fer a drink so I may convince ye to stay!"

"Forgive my ignorance, but I dinna think ye can persuade me, e'en wit yer finest whisky," Bram smiled in return.

"Och, only a fool would turn down such a noble position. At least join me fer the bloody drink," John interjected.

Bram looked to Lara.

"Tis fine. I will be here when ye and my brother return. I had hoped to speak to King Eric and Queen Isobel, mayhap now is a good time to do so," Lara said.

Bram followed John down a long winding corridor, then down a flight of stairs at the end of the hall. The stairs were narrow, and reminded Bram of the staircase at Dunakin Castle that the servants used when cleaning and bringing up buckets of water to fill the tubs. The stairs led to a cellar room, where cartons were stacked along a wall and shelves were filled with bottles.

"Whisky!" Bram exclaimed, as he picked up one of the dusty bottles to examine it.

"Aye. The inhabitants of the castle store their best wine and whisky down here. They were distilled by the local monks. They only serve the watered down jugs to their guests, and keep the strong and rich-tasting ones fer themselves. It's cool down here, so it makes the stuff taste even better," John explained, as he grabbed one of the dusty bottles of whiskey and opened it, taking a big swig.

"When do ye hope to return to Scotland?"

"I had planned to return soon."

"Ye have been a great service to my sister. Tis too bad ye will nay reconsider my offer. I am sure ye will be sadly missed," John said, as he picked up a heavy red bottle from the shelf.

"Truth is, I wish to marry her."

"Marry? Well, that does change things a bit." John cocked his head to the side. "Shh…did ye hear something?"

Bram quieted his movements, listening for the sound John had referred to. Turning around to look at the other end of the room, Bram heard a shuffle. Before he knew it, he was hit over the head with a hard object. He took one step forward to regain his balance before everything turned black. Bram fumbled and went crashing down onto the cold dirt floor.

Lara sat on the edge of her chair for several long moments before speaking to her father. Looking at his features, she could see many similarities to her own.

Chewing on her bottom lip, she tapped him on the shoulder to gain his attention.

"My Lord, I was wondering, I hoped to…" Lara stuttered. Even though he was her father, he was still a King.

"Lara, I had hoped to speak to you as well. Will you join me?" he asked, standing up and holding his arm out to her.

Lara hesitantly took it and folded her arm around his. Together, they walked to the library.

"Lara, ye are heiress to the throne of Norway. It is both your duty and your right. This is your home now if you wish to stay."

Lara smiled and replied, "I wish it verra much. I have so many questions to ask I just dinna ken where to start."

Eric sat down on the chair adjacent to her, and regaled her with stories about his past, her mother and all of the events that led up to now. He explained that his illness was an untreatable lung ailment, and that the healers believed he had little time left; a year, perhaps two.

"Lara, ye are my legacy. When I perish, I know that my blood runs through you, and because of that I will live on forever."

His bittersweet words brought tears to Lara's eyes. Eric stood from his chair and gathered Lara into his arms, wiping her tears away. Her whole life, this was all she'd ever asked from the man she thought was her father. To be loved as a father should love his daughter.

Lara returned to the great hall, waiting for John and Bram to return. But hours had passed and there were still no signs of them. John was a gambling man, and had been known to drink himself into a stupor, so it was plausible that they were out somewhere doing something reckless. But what didn't make sense was that no one else seemed to know where they were. As King, he would have guards on watch for protection. Would John really be naïve enough to go off alone?

Much like a rabbit, Lara nervously began eating a slice of apple, taking several tiny bites at a time. She wasn't even hungry, but she needed to fidget with something to distract herself, and the apple was the only object she could find. Had she her needles and thread, she could have stitched an entire tapestry in the time that she waited. Finally, Lara stood and thought it best to wait upstairs in her chamber. Perhaps they would come for her there.

Chapter 24

With his eyes closed, Bram examined the bump on the top of his head. His hair felt wet. Was he bleeding?

"Bloody hell," he said out loud, as he opened his eyes and looked down at his hand. The liquid was bright red, but did not ooze like blood. Bringing his hand up to his noise, he smelled the sweet smell of red wine. Someone had hit him over the head with one of the bottles, he presumed, continuing to rub the lump on the side of his head.

Remembering that he was not alone, he called out, "John," hoping to hear his friend, but no one responded. Bram staggered to his feet. Had someone tried to kill him and take John prisoner? Bram searched every nook and corner of the room from which he thought the attacker had come. Bram felt as if he had been kicked in the stomach, and his nerves felt like pins and needles. He ran out of the room, taking the stairs two at a time. He was desperate to get to Lara, for he knew now that she was still in grave danger.

❧

Lara stepped inside her room and closed the door behind her. She hoped that her brother and Bram would return soon. As she began to turn around, someone grabbed her from behind and firmly pressed a dagger to her throat. Lara was too afraid to scream or struggle with the sharp end of the blade pressed so close to her throat. If this person wanted her dead, they easily could have killed her. The hold on her was strong and almost painful as he pressed his arm tightly against her stomach. Pulling her away from the light of the window, he turned her around and pushed her up against the wall, keeping the dagger against her throat.

Lara stared into the familiarity of his icy blue eyes. So stricken with fear, she struggled to breathe. Her stomach felt sick and for a moment, she thought she would collapse to the ground. After all this time, she was certain that it was Dermot and her father who had betrayed her, but neither stood before her, holding a dagger to her throat. It was John.

"It was ye! The French gypsy woman, the men hunting me in the village, the English guards at Cumberland, ye planned this whole thing. Why?" Lara bellowed.

"Because ye were the true royal heir to the crown."

His words crushed her like boulders. She could barely breathe enough to form a sentence or two. Lara felt bile rising in her throat.

"So all of this, the lies, the deceit, it was about the crown?"

John chuckled.

"Ye poor silly lass. Ye ken nothing of what power can bring ye. With me as King, I can now lead a great army, more powerful than England or France."

"Did father ken?"

"Nay, the foolish ol' mon. He was just as daft and ignorant as ye are. Would have killed him myself, had he no' already gotten himself at the end of the noose."

"Ye will no' get away wit' this, John."

Whispering in her ear, his voice became chilling. "I already have. And now that I got rid of Laird Moray and that Highland friend of yers, there is no one to stand in me way."

"Bram," Lara's voice weakened. "What have ye done?"

"Only the same thing I am going to do to ye. My wee sister; so upset that her Highland warrior left that she could no' go on living. 'Tis a shame, yer death. I promise ye will be mourned and will have a Christian burial."

"Ye sick and wicked mon," Lara yelled, and tried to break free from his grasp.

As John tilted his head back and laughed, Lara kicked him in the groin, causing him to drop the dagger. Lara successfully jerked herself out of his hold, ran to the door, and tried to open it, but it was locked from the inside. Lara ran to the corner of the room, searching for something to use as a weapon. She was trapped like a mouse. She began picking up random objects around the room, throwing them in John's direction and aiming for his head. But he kept stalking towards her.

Before Lara could scream, John had her pinned down to the ground, bumping the back of her head on the floor. She tried to break free, she tried to push him off of her, but it was no use. John was too big and too heavy.

Bram jiggled the locked door handle to Lara's room, hearing the commotion going on behind it. With one powerful kick, he burst through the door and immediately tackled John to the ground. Within moments, John had Bram pinned down, his hands wrapped around his throat. As Bram struggled to kick John off of him, he noticed the dagger on the floor just a few feet away from him. Bram reached as far as he could to grab the dagger. With the tips of his fingers, he dragged it closer to him until he could firmly grip the handle. Bringing the dagger up, he plunged it into John's back. John's lifeless body collapsed to the floor. Bram pulled his legs from where they were buried underneath the dead man's body, freeing himself.

On his knees, he crawled over to where Lara was lying on the floor. He began assessing her wounds, even though Lara protested. Never had he been so scared of losing someone before, and he never wanted to feel that way again. Still lying on the floor, Bram hovered over her. Lara's sterling eyes sparkled like the sun reflecting off polished metal. His feelings for her were as strong as steel. Lowering his lips to hers, he kissed her with all his heart and soul.

"Ach, what is the meaning of this?" a guard said, standing in the doorway with mouth agape. "You, you killed the young King." In a high pitched voice the man yelled out, "Guards, guards."

Suddenly, a group of armed men came running from down the hallway and piled into the bedchamber. Grabbing Bram by his arm pits, lifting him to his feet, two of the guards held him firmly while the other two grabbed onto Lara.

"Dinna hurt her," Bram roared, trying to break free.

"You just wait until King Eric hears about your treachery, you murderous bastard," one of the guards holding him stated in a deep and stern, tone as he punched Bram square in the stomach, hoping to weaken him further.

"Bram!" Lara yelled out.

"What the bloody hell is going on?" Eric bellowed, his voice booming so loud everyone fell silent.

"This man killed King John," a guard replied.

Eric looked beyond the group of them to John's lifeless body. His face showed no expression, but when he turned to see the two guards who had apprehended Lara, Eric's heavy-lidded eyes narrowed.

With his brow furrowed and lips pursed, he demanded, "Release my daughter. That is an order."

The guards looked at each other as if the King had gone daft. For what they knew, the King's only daughter was a bairn of no more than one year old. They stood as if they were frozen like a statue. They simply just did not know what to think.

"I said release her," Eric roared louder.

The two guards holding Lara quickly let go.

"And you can release him as well," he said, nodding his head in Bram's direction.

"But Sir," one of the other guards said, but snapped his mouth shut at the dark expression Eric turned on him.

"I will settle this mess. Now leave us."

The four guards looked at each other before leaving the room, clearly confused by their king's behavior.

As they left, Eric closed the door and asked, "What happened here?" His question was directed to Bram, but it was Lara who spoke up first.

"Father, dinna blame Bram. John tried to kill me. He knew all along that I was yer daughter but wanted the throne fer himself. He was the one behind all of the lies and deception. I fear that if Bram had not stopped him, he would have killed ye and Queen Isobel as well."

Eric searched her eyes and knew she spoke the truth. "Then, you have done me and my country a great service. I don't know how I can ever repay you for saving my daughter."

Bram stepped forward and kneeled down before him.

"I only ask one thing, my Lord. I wish fer yer daughter's hand in marriage. If she will have me," Bram asked, more nervous than he had ever felt before.

Knots formed in his stomach and his mouth felt dry. Wringing his hands together he anxiously waited for a reply.

"Will ye marry me, lass," he asked looking back over to a stunned, wide-eyed Lara.

"Nay," she whispered.

Bram's sweet demeanor was quickly replaced by bitter rejection. That was not the response he had expected.

"I want to, but I can no' marry ye. If I were to marry ye, I would have to leave here. I have just only met my father two days ago and with his illness, I may no' have much time left wit' him."

Bram's heart ached. He wanted Lara more than anything he had ever wanted.

"Then I guess ye leave me nay choice," he responded.

Both Eric and Lara looked at him in utter confusion. Lara could feel a lump beginning to form in the back of her throat. She truly wanted to marry Bram, but her heart was pulled in two different directions. Lara felt as if he had just ripped her heart right out of her chest. But she wanted him to have it, to take it with him and know that she would forever and always love him.

"I will just have to stay here, then. But ye will marry me, that is, of course, if I may have yer blessing," he said turning to Eric, trying to hold back his smile.

"I would be most honored, Bram MacKinnon, to call you my son," Eric replied.

Lara leaped towards Bram and jumped into his arms. Bram lifted her up and swung her around, as Eric laughed at their youthful affectionate display.

Chapter 25

In a private ceremony, Lara and Bram exchanged vows. Bram did not want a wedding with many guests he did not know. Plus, it did not feel right without his brother or mother being there. He rather preferred the quiet intimacy of a small wedding with only those who needed to be there present, though he did consent to the Queen and King joining them in their celebration. Bram found it hard to say no to her, which was something he promised himself he would work on. He most certainly couldn't have a lass ordering him around as though he were a lovesick puppy, obeying her every command.

As the priest announced them man and wife, Bram kissed her quickly, eager to take his new bride to their bedchamber. He did not want to wait any longer. Disappointment shot threw him like a kick to the groin, as Queen Isobel announced she had planned a celebratory meal. On the table within the great hall were platters full of roasted lamb and venison.

King Eric made a toast. "May the light find you in your darkest hours, may your home be filled with love and laughter, and may your life be full of many sweet babes. Let us eat and rejoice at this delightful celebration."

The four of them raised their mugs and drank their bittersweet wine. As quickly as he could, Bram cleared his plate. Having a quick bite would only help increase his stamina. He knew that he was going to need all of the energy he had this night, for he planned on taking his wife more than once before the night was through.

As they finished their meal, Bram held out his arm to Lara. Excusing their early departure, they walked out of the great hall hand in hand.

"By the saints, if that damn room was no' three flights up the stairs," Bram growled as he picked Lara up in his arms and ran up the stairs two steps at a time. He did not want to wait another minute.

Bram carried Lara over the threshold and into their bedchamber. Tonight, he would show her pleasures she never thought possible, and he couldn't get her into the room fast enough. His body ached with need, and though he did not know how long this night would last, he would take his time with her, to kiss and explore every inch of her soft creamy body.

As they entered the room, Bram closed the door behind him and set her down gently onto the floor. Forcefully, he pushed her up against the back of the door. Pressing his body against hers, he lowered his head and caught her lips. As he swept his tongue inside her mouth, Lara moaned.

Dropping to one bent knee, Bram slid he hands down her sides, around her hips and the full length of her legs. The fingers of one hand crawled up her leg under her skirt. He could hear the sound of Lara's breath increase as his hand glided further north. With one hand firmly pressing on the back of her rump, he moved the other to the crevice between her legs. His fingers pushed past the apex of her thighs and slid one finger inside of her velvety wet skin.

Lara almost yelled aloud, but Bram hushed her, reminding her of the servants, and their propensity for eavesdropping. As he touched her most private parts, sparks of light flashed before her eyes and tiny vibrations sent tremors throughout her body. Wobbling at the knees, she felt as if she could barely have stood in one place had it not been for Bram's hand holding her backside steady. As he fondled her down below, her hips involuntarily rocked, increasing his momentum.

As her body reached the height of her climax, she started to pant. Suddenly, a burst of pleasure exploded inside of her, causing her to body to quiver. Bram slid his hand back down her leg and fixed the bottom of her skirt so it draped down as it should. Standing up, he once again kissed her before lifting her into his arms.

"That was…" Lara said, still trying to catch her breath.

"Aye. And that was only the beginning," he replied, nuzzling his nose in her hair along her neck. "Lara, I ne'er want to lose ye," he whispered, kissing the side of her mouth, down her cheek, and trailing even further down, stopping at the base of her neck. "I want ye, always," he said as he continued devouring her neck like a hungry wolf.

Lara took small shuffling steps backwards leading Bram towards the bed. As she gently sat on the edge, she reached up and grabbed the collar of his shirt and pulled him down to kiss her. Softly, she bit his bottom lip as her hands rubbed down his hard chest, stopping just above his belt line.

Scooting herself higher up the bed, she lay down, waiting for Bram to join her. With a roguish smile, he walked to the far end of the bed.

With a tender touch he slipped off her slippers one at a time, and began rubbing the soles of her feet. Massaging his rough hand down the sides of her smooth legs, he caressed her left calf, kissing from her ankle to the top of her knee. Pulling his tunic over his head, he dropped it to the floor, followed by his boots and kilt.

Climbing up onto the bed, he eased himself between her thighs and hovered over her. Looking into her silvery eyes, he knew he was looking into the face of his future. With heavy breaths, his lips captured hers. Thrusting his hands onto her body, he caressed her breasts with a feverish need to touch them. Wanting to feel her skin pressed up against his own, he playfully pulled the laces of her dress loosening the top. Pulling the fabric down exposing her breasts, he teased her small buds with the tip of his nose. He growled deeply in the back of his throat when he heard a trembling sigh escape Lara's lips.

Murmuring against her lips, he whispered, "Lass, ye can make a man die just from wantin' ye."

Lara smiled at his remark but there was more truth behind what he said than she could imagine. With heat searing through his veins and his manhood pulsating against her velvety skin he could very well have completed the task before they even began the coupling. Licking and tasting her sweet skin enticed him. His hands moved about her body as if they had a mind of their own, though Lara did not once complain. In fact, he believed she rather enjoyed the sweet caresses.

Hearing his seductive voice made Lara more eager for his hands to be on her body. Raising her arms, she waited as Bram lifted the dress from her. The soft fabric tickled her skin as he gently removed her gown and tossed it on the floor.

As Bram nestled himself back between her thighs, Lara's chest heaved with anticipation. Overwhelming sensations exploded throughout her body as she clutched onto him. As Bram cupped a hand around her breast, she felt a sudden awareness of an aching need between her thighs pulsing as he pressed his manhood against her. Arching her back and raising her hips, her body welcomed his. As Bram thrust his manhood forward, Lara let out a scream. The pain shot through her like a lightning bolt as it resonated through her body.

"Are ye alright?" Bram asked, lifting himself off her.

"I dinna ken. Does it always hurt like this yer first time?"

"First time? Do ye mean to tell me that ye are a virgin?"

"Aye."

"But, ye were married. I thought that ye…"

"Nay. We never consummated."

Bram had never bedded a virgin before. Somehow the fact that Lara had not shared a bed with another man made Bram feel more possessive of her. He felt terrible that he had caused her pain, for if he knew she was a virgin he could have taken care and been gentle with her. Not wanting to hurt her any longer he slid up beside her.

"Nay, dinna stop."

"I dinna want to hurt ye, lass."

"I am feeling better now."

"Are ye sure?"

At her nod, Bram rolled back between her legs and slowly eased himself inside her. He held his body still for her pain to subside before gently rocking his hips back and forth. Lara moaned from the sensations. The pleasure she felt was almost unbearable.

The way he made her feel brought tears to her eyes. She felt as if she soared above the heavens and only Bram could keep her grounded and bring her back down. The friction between them matched their heated passion. As Bram increased the motion of his hips, he pressed harder and further inside of her causing a distinct feeling to build within her very core.

Sensations intensified as her body convulsed underneath him. Matching his tempo, she raised her legs and crawled higher to allow him better access. When her almost indescribable pleasure increased, she felt her body quiver causing her to tighten her hold onto him. Lara moaned loudly. After her release, the height of her orgasm started to decline and her breathing slowed. With Bram's body pressed tight against hers she could feel his manhood throbbing inside of her as he climaxed and emptied his seed within her womb.

Slick with sweat, Bram rolled himself off of Lara and snuggled up behind her, keeping her tightly in his arms. With a ridiculous smile on his face, he pressed tiny butterfly kisses on the base of her neck, causing Lara to giggle. He wanted to give Lara every pleasure imaginable. By God, he loved this woman. This night had been one of the best nights he had ever had and he was determined to make each night with her better than the last.

Lara felt as if her smile would forever be painted on her face. She had never thought that what could happen between a man and a woman would be so intense and satisfying. She had always thought that bedding was only meant to produce bairns, but never did she think that she would actually enjoy her husband's attention. *Her husband.* In all her wildest dreams, she never imagined her marriage to be a love match, and had she been forced to stay wed to Dermot she never would have experienced the wonders that Bram had shown her this night.

As she cuddled in his arms, she asked, "What of tomorrow? Will ye send a messenger to yer family, or retrieve yer lads?"

"Nay, I had hoped in a few months that we would travel there together. I wish fer ye to meet my family and me lads."

"I would be forever glad to meet yer family."

"I must warn ye, though. The MacKinnons are a hellish bunch of drunken, loud men. But ye will ne'er find yerself a clan wit more honor."

Lara giggled. "I suppose I should have met them first before marrying ye. If all of the Highlanders are anything like ye, I could have verra well married the wrong one," she playfully teased.

Bram's lips twisted.

"Ach, ye lowland women, yer all the same. Stubborn."

"Well then best ye take me again before I change my mind."

Chapter 26

Four months later...

The winter in Norway had been brutal, one of the worst they had seen according to Queen Isobel. Hard-packed powder buried the village in three feet of snow, barricading doors and blocking several well-traveled roads. Villagers spent weeks clearing paths from nature's winter fury. Lara and Bram had to wait until the snowcaps on the mountains melted before they could travel back to Scotland.

As the days and weeks went by, early signs of spring started to show. Lara and Bram packed their belongings and sailed back across the ocean towards Scottish soil with a chest full of coin and a new Norwegian ally.

For several days they rode across the Highlands towards Lara's new home at Dunakin Castle. Nerves pricked under her skin at the thought of meeting Bram's clan. One Highlander she could manage, but a whole clan of them was something entirely different.

Heavy spring rain fell with intense fury, causing several unexpected delays. But Lara did not mind so much, as each night Bram would make sweet and passionate love to her and hold her throughout the night to keep her warm. Since Adam and Eve, no two souls had ever connected so strongly, and proof of their love was evident by the bairn in her womb.

Lara knew she was with child when her monthly flow had not come in weeks, but she kept the secret to herself until she could find the perfect time to reveal her condition to Bram.

After several days travel during the treacherous storm, the sky had finally cleared. By early morning, the surrounding landmarks became more familiar to Bram as they rode towards his home. Excitement filled his heart when he knew within minutes he would be looking down on his village and castle. As they reached the edge of the hill, from his position high on the mountain peak, the sight of Dunakin Castle caused a sense of comfort to wash over Bram like a rainstorm. Never had he been more excited to be home. *Home.* Just the sight of it brought a smile to his face. The anticipation of seeing the smiles on his two young lad's tiny faces had almost bought a tear to his eye.

The castle looked to be exactly the same as when he left almost nine months ago, not that he had expected the walls to be caved in or the keep to be badly destroyed. After all, he knew his brother and cousin could manage well without him, though the three of them had been inseparable.

The horse trotted slowly down the rocky mountainside as it pulled the cart with their belongings. Draped with a thick black cloak, Bram's return was not apparent to anyone they had passed in the village, but his first priority was reuniting with his family.

As they rode into the courtyard of Dunakin Castle, Bram spotted his two lads sitting on the ground with a bonny fair-haired lass who appeared to be heavy wit child. He watched them for a moment before he directed his horse in their direction. Butterflies swarmed in the pit of his stomach.

Dismounting the horse, he asked, "Excuse me, lass. Do ye ken if Laird MacKinnon is within the keep?"

"Yes, he is," she replied stepping away from the children to greet him.

Bram almost lost his footing by the lass's English accent. What in bloody hell would an

English lass be doing here and playing with *his* lads of all things?

"Who are ye?" he questioned in a demanding tone.

"My name is Jacqueline. And may I have the honor of your name, Sir?" Jacqueline asked, not liking the way he looked at her.

Bram raised his eyebrow at the outspoken Englishwoman.

"I'm a MacKinnon that is who I bloody am."

"A MacKinnon? Then ye must be related to my husband, Ewan," she said as she nodded her head past Bram towards the stables.

"Ewan? Yer husband?" Bram almost fell over in laughter at the woman's statement.

"How dare ye talk to my wife that way?" Ewan asked from behind him. Bram knew his voice instantly.

Bram turned, keeping his hood up, covering his face.

"Ewan, of all people. Married to an Englishwoman. I guess ye did say there was nay a lass in all of Scotland who could tame ye."

Ewan's jaw dropped as Bram lowered his cloak.

"Bram!" Ewan exclaimed as he wrapped his arms around him. "Yer alive!"

"Aye, but I will nay be much longer if ye dinna loosen yer grip around my neck," Bram choked out. Ewan released him, but kept his hand firmly on his shoulder.

"What happened to ye? Where have ye been? I thought ye were dead. Had I known, I swear I would ne'er have…," Ewan asked.

"Tis a long story, cousin, but first I wish to see my lads and my brother and mother. I can regale all of ye wit my journey over a warm meal," Bram said reassuring him.

"Well dinna just stand there, come inside, ye fool."

Bram turned and headed back to his horse, where Lara was still perched, watching the joyous reunion. Holding his hand up to her, he helped her off the horse.

"Ewan, I would like ye to meet, Lara. My wife."

The expression painted on Ewan's face as Lara came into view went from pleasant to jaw-dropping astonishment.

"Wife? So after all this time and all the lassies ye finally found one and settled down."

"Aye, I did."

Colin and Connor dropped the toys they were playing with and ran in between both Ewan and Bram.

"Da?" Colin cried out.

Bram smiled down at the two teary-eyed boys. Both lads leapt from the ground and jumped into Bram's arms. The sound of tears and laughter warmed Lara's heart. It was delightful to witness such affection from a father to his sons. It made missing her father all the more painful, but she was glad for the short time she had with him.

Bram held Lara's arm and followed Ewan, Jacqueline and the lads inside the keep.

Lara leaned towards him and asked, "All the lassies?" Repeating what Ewan had said. "Just how many lassies have ye shared yer bed wit?"

Bram bit his lower lip, unsure how to answer. He had lost count ages ago, but did not want to admit that little truth.

"Ah, a few," he replied.

As they entered into the great hall, a flock of women crowded around him, calling out his name and pawing at him like they were crows pecking at their meal. Lara crossed her arms and could not believe the scene before her eyes. Bram tried to escape them but the women followed him like flies.

"Only a few?" Lara loudly asked, staring daggers at the women who swarmed around her husband.

"Ladies, some dignity, please," Bram said, successfully pushing himself away from the group of women and moving to stand next to Lara. With a trying-to-be-innocent look plastered on his face, he twisted his lips, waiting for Lara to thrash him. Lara curled her lips and gave him that "just wait till later" look.

The group of women pouted as they saw Bram wrap his arm around Lara's and escort her into the next room. Lara walked slowly and with dignity, hoping to appear as a threat. Inwardly, she smiled.

Bram glanced around the room expecting to see his brother sitting at the head table and his mother sitting by the fire attending to her needlework, but the room was vacant. After a few short moments, the kitchen door swung open as though blown by a furious wind. His brother Rory filled the doorframe. He looked at Bram as if he could not believe his eyes. It took only moments until he ran towards him and wrapped his younger brother in such a tight embrace that Bram could barely breathe from his grip.

With Rory's forehead pressed to Bram's, he said to him, "My brother has returned from the grave and has come home." Looking into his eyes, Rory pleaded, "Why? Why did ye leave? Ye dinna have to go into battle. I had sent plenty of our men. I did no' mean fer ye to go. Please forgive me, if ye thought any different. I ne'er would have wished fer it. No' fer my only brother to put himself into danger. We thought ye were dead. Poor Ewan has been heavily weighed by guilt o'er it. He blamed himself, as did I. Forgive me, brother."

Bram placed his hands on the sorrowful man's shoulders.

"Ye have nay reason to be burdened by guilt, brother. 'Twas no' yer fault or doing that I left. I went on my own behalf and of my own doing. It was where I belonged, on the battlefield, no' here. Dunakin is where ye belong. Ye are Laird of this clan, and this clan needs their leader. My only regret is that I did no' kill enough of those bloody bastards before they rendered me unconscious," Bram replied, ending in sarcasm.

"Well, ye are home now. Mother will be most pleased. She has mourned yer death every day since Ewan returned wit' the news."

"Rory, I would like ye to meet Lara, my wife. Lara, this is my brother, Laird Rory MacKinnon, Laird of Dunakin Castle."

"Wife? Well, my lady, ye have my congratulations, and I welcome ye to the family, though I must say ye have questionable taste in men," Rory said jokingly.

"Thank ye. But I can promise ye yer brother is a kind and honest gentlemen."

Ewan leaned into Rory and whispered, "I knew it! She's daft. No woman in her right mind would think of Bram as gentle!"

The two of them laughed until tears filled their eyes. Bram squeezed his brows together, creasing his forehead and stared at them angrily as they openly whispered to one another, giving him a reason to toss each one of them over his shoulder and knock them on their arse. Not that he'd ever needed a reason before.

Rory's laughter broke. "Tonight, we will feast in honor of my brother's return," he announced.

Chapter 27

As Bram gave Lara a tour of the castle grounds, it looked exactly as Bram had described it. Floral tapestries hung on the walls, and the rooms smelled of fresh rushes and lilac. Wooden rockers sat before a giant hearth in the great hall with needles and unfinished blankets folded over the arm of the chair as if someone had not quite finished the stitching. And in the hearth, a roaring fire blazed, keeping the first floor of the castle warm and comforting.

Overall, the castle folk were very welcoming and very different than where she grew up at Stearns Castle. Lara was grateful for Rory's generous hospitality and the warm greetings she received from Bram's clansmen. With each person they passed, more and more people expressed their happiness for Bram's return.

Every thought and assumption she had about the Highlanders, she realized, was wrong. Her only accurate preconception about them was that they were indeed tall and fierce, though they were also kind and friendly. Lara looked forward to beginning her tasks around the castle helping the women, and starting her new life here.

Excitedly, Colin and Connor helped Bram with the tour, showing Lara all of their favorite places to play and hide, as well as where they lived in the village. Lara was surprised to know that the two boys were only half-brothers, and did not live within the castle. But their homes with their mothers were close to the castle grounds, and they could see Bram whenever they wanted.

As they walked around the grounds, they entered the burial grounds of the church. A chill shook Bram causing the hairs on the back of his neck to stand. Along the path next to his father was a fresh grave marked with a slab of stone - *his* grave. It only made sense that they would have made a grave stone for him and placed it next to his father's since they had believed he was dead, but seeing his own stone was too surreal and it made him uncomfortable. Bram's first task at hand would be to make sure the stone was removed until the day when it would be needed again.

By mid-day the kitchen staff had created a plentiful feast with enough food to fill every belly. Minstrels played their instruments while others ate, drank and danced away into the evening hours. Throughout the entire day, Bram could not take his eyes off his wife. She was absolutely glowing. Lara had worn the blue silk dress he had bought her, which made him smile.

Bram grabbed Lara's hand and dragged her away from the crowd into a private alcove within the hallway. Bram brushed her hair to the side and pressed his body close to hers.

"How would ye like the tour of our room now?" he asked, as he started kissing her neck and nibbling on her ear.

Lara softly moaned. How could she refuse? Bram took her moan as affirmation and led her up the stairs. The bedchamber they were to share was only one floor up, and he thanked the heavens for the short distance.

Bram opened the door to his room and escorted Lara inside. The first room they entered was the solar. The room was an unorganized and disorderly mess. On top of a dusty wooden desk were stacks of books and papers, and in the corner of the room were two chairs next to a small fireplace. Lara made a mental note to clean and organize the room when her time permitted.

Turning to face him, Lara wrapped her arms around Bram's neck and planted several tiny kisses all over his face.

"I love ye," Lara whispered in his ear.

"I love ye too, Lass, but if ye dinna stop now I may have to take ye right here on the floor, and I haven't even shown ye the rest of the room."

"Then ye better get to showing me to the bed," Lara replied, with a teasing tone in her voice.

An arched doorway led them into the bedchamber. In the middle of the room was a large wooden bed draped in several blankets and plaids. Feather-stuffed pillows rested along the headboard. On the far end of the room was a dresser that matched the carvings of the headboard and a full, walk-in wardrobe.

"I have never seen such a large bedchamber before. I suppose 'tis a decent size; wit the bairn and all, we will need the extra room," Lara remarked as she waited for Bram's reaction to her news.

"Bairn!"

Bram looked down at her stomach and then back to her. He hadn't realized she was wit' child, though he should have known. They had made love almost every night, and not once did he recall her monthly bleeding. A wide smile grew on his face. "Well, what are ye doing standing there? Ye should lie down or something."

Lara laughed at his ridiculous suggestion.

"Bram, I'm pregnant, not bed-ridden!" Lara looked around the bedchamber. "I think the room is perfect," she responded, admiring the space they were to share together as a family.

Bram reached out for Lara and pulled her close.

"Nay lass," he said placing a kiss on her forehead. "Ye are."

The End

Author's Notes

For purposes of the story I had to change a few events and details. In regards to King Eric Magnusson II, Eric Magnusson was King of Norway from 1280 until his death in 1299. He was succeeded by his brother Haakon V. During his reign, he waged war with Denmark from 1287 until 1295.

His marriage to Margaret of Scotland ended in 1283 when she died during the birth of their child Maid Margaret, Queen of the Scots. Maid Margaret died in 1290 while traveling to Scotland. His second wife was Isobel Bruce from 1293 until his death in 1299. More information can be found in the Lanercost Chronicles, details found on this website: https://archive.org/details/chronicleoflaner00max wuoft. Information can also be found on Wikipedia, though some information may not be reliable.

The Battle of Falkirk took place on 22 July 1298. The battle was against the English. The Scots were led by William Wallace.

More information can be found on the following website: http://www.battlefieldstrust.com/resource-centre/medieval/battleview.asp?BattleFieldId=62. Information can also be found on Wikipedia, though, again, some information may not be reliable.

The MacKinnon Clan Series
Book One:
The Honor of a Highlander

Laird Rory MacKinnon sets out to join William Wallace after discovering an imminent threat that the English have planned an attack. Raised as a warrior, he has given his heart and soul to fight for Scotland's freedom, until he meets a lass who captures his heart like no other, Lady Annella. After learning of a brutal attack on her land by the English, Rory discovers that Annella has been taken prisoner by the English. Now Rory must fight; not only to secure his own clan's freedom but to save the woman he loves.

Annella, the eldest daughter of the MacCallum clan, vows never to marry, until the day Rory MacKinnon enters her life and opens her heart. She knew, though, that with Rory heading off to war, there was no future for them. After her father offers aid to Laird MacKinnon and his men to help in their campaign, her castle is attacked and her father is killed by the English for treason. Starved and beaten for denying her allegiance to the English King, Annella has earned her place on the gallows. Her fate now rests in Rory's hands.

The MacKinnon Clan Series
Book Two:
Escape to the Highlands:

Her enemy was the only one she could trust...

Jacqueline Renold, an English born lady, is the sister to the king's executioner. In love with one man and forced to marry another, she feels no different than the prisoners below in the dungeons. After witnessing one too many Scots hung by the noose, she makes a decision that will change her life. She frees the prisoners. Knowing her actions are treasonous, she flees to Scotland with a bounty on her head...

Ewan, the Laird's cousin, is second in command of their army. Third in line to the MacKinnon Clan, he has no home or land of his own, only the sword on his back. Through his skill as a warrior, he seeks out to find his place in the world. Ewan travels south with William Wallace to help free those who the English have been taking captive. But when duty and honor lead Ewan to help an English lass in grave danger, the last thing he expects is to lose his heart to his enemy.

Dear Readers:

Thank you for joining me in this adventure of the MacKinnon Clan. I have immensely enjoyed writing it and have fallen in love with these characters. As this has been my first published series, I look forward to writing more books and taking you on more adventures with other Scottish Clans and honorable heroes. Thank you again for your support!

~April Holthaus

About the Author

April lives in central Minnesota with her husband and son. April developed her passion of historical romances through her love of history and genealogy. Over the last several years she has compiled her family tree finding over 350 bloodline grandparents dating back to the 1100s.
April is very passionate about history and nature. When she is not working or writing, April loves to spend her free time outdoors and with her family.

For more information about April Holthaus and her upcoming books please follow her at:

www.facebook.com/author.april.holthaus
https://twitter.com/AprilHolthaus

Made in the USA
Charleston, SC
10 January 2015